DRINKING DRY CLOUDS

DRINKING DRY CLOUDS

Stories from Wyoming

GRETEL EHRLICH

CAPRA PRESS
SANTA BARBARA

In memory of
Joel Grabbert
Smokey Grabbert
Grady Stead
and especially
"Mike" Tisdale Hinckley

Library of Congress Cataloging-in-Publication Data
Ehrlich, Gretel.
  Drinking dry clouds, Wyoming stories / Gretel Ehrlich
    p. cm.
  ISBN 0-88496-315-2 $9.95
  1. Wyoming—Fiction. I. Title.
PS3555.H72D75   1991
813'.54—dc20   90-19862
                                                                              CIP

CAPRA PRESS
Post Office Box 2068
Santa Barbara, CA 93120

C O N T E N T S

FOREWORD

These linked stories were written in the winter of
1989–1990. They are preceded by a novel, *Heart Mountain*, which was the outgrowth of the first set of stories
in this volume. When I returned to my characters, five
years after their initial appearance in my life, they
seemed to want to report to me, so I let them speak in
the first person. These stories are brief, like the palm-in-
the-hand stories Yasunari Kawabata compiled, small
enough to hold in the palm of your hand, yet I hope that
if you open your fingers they will fly.

G.E.

Heart Mountain, Wyoming

1990

PART I:

During the War

1

PINKEY

ACROSS THE ROAD from the bar a calcium mine spewed pink dust that drifted across the state line into Wyoming. Two front-end loaders, a long wooden shed, and three cars on a railroad siding were dusted pink and for a mile thickets of greasewood and sagebrush, leaning south away from shouldering winds, caught the mined chalk as did the cattle that grazed there.

A sorrel horse was tied between two pickups at the bar. With her back leg cocked, her whole body looked crooked. One rein dangled straight down from the bit into the mud. Someone had written "Ride me" in the dust that covered the saddle.

Soon enough those words were obliterated by falling snow. It was snow from a storm that had hit Pinkey's camp then proceeded east across rugged grazing land, the clouds fanning out in the miles between towns like a skirt being lengthened.

"All bad weather starts here," Pinkey had said to himself. It was not winter yet and he shook his head in disgust. He had ridden through fifty years of storms, cow-boying on yearling outfits in Nevada, cow-calf operations in Montana, and for the last twelve years he had worked for the young McKay. He put on his overshoes and coat, cut the wires on a bale of hay he had used as a couch all summer and fed a third of it to his mare. He looked up. He heard the drone of a plane but could see nothing. The sky like the ground was white. Yesterday it had been purely blue. One cloud had passed overhead. It was shaped like a human penis and rode the airwaves erect, pointing heavenward, Pinkey had thought, so now his usual, nuisance, morning erection, ordinarily reminding him of his solitary state, became something blessed. For a whole summer Pinkey had looked out on tall grass swinging back and forth in the wind. Now snow rolled over the range. Once, after too much booze, he thought the grass was a bed of seaweed—rubbery, thick, cold—and he was trapped beneath it, bobbing for air.

He went back to bed. When he woke again he was cold. He looked outside and it occurred to him that yesterday's phallic cloud had softened and drained and come apart like cooked meat into the white smithereens falling on him as snow.

* * *

12

Pinkey was not in the bar where his horse was tied. Hours before he had hitched a ride into a town on the Wyoming side of the line. He cashed a paycheck saved from a summer at linecamp and bought himself new wool pants, a shirt and a winter jacket. In the store he looked at himself in the mirror. Next to the salesman, a big Mormon man who doubled as the undertaker, Pinkey looked small. His short legs bowed, he was toothless, and from his cracked lips a line of blood drove down his chin and dripped on the floor.

He went to the bars. "Drinks for the house!" he said in each one, though "the house" rarely consisted of more than two or three old men — sheepherders or cowboys too bunged up to work — plus the bartenders who rarely drank at ten in the morning so early in what Pinkey called "the drinking year" which began when the weather turned cold.

*   *   *

Snow fell throughout the basin. It filled the great draws and softened tumbled breaks, and the long lines of rimrock hemming the mountains above McKay's ranch shone orange. Breaking tree branches had awakened McKay. They fell against the house in sharp reports as if to remind him there was a war on. He needed none. A bad dream had awakened him earlier. He was in a hospital on the front line looking for his brothers. Room after room was filled with bodies stacked up. Their heads and limbs had been cut off and the torsos were tied together in bundles like newspapers. That's how they were sent home.

Of three brothers, McKay was the one who could not pass an Army physical because one leg, crushed in a horse accident, was still weak and considerably shorter than the other. Naked, he limped out to the screened porch. He thought it was wind that had caused the cottonwood limbs to break, then he saw the snow. he was more legs than torso and his reedlike body was as pale and graceful as a Sandhill Crane's. Snow sifted sideways through the mesh and chilled him. This would bring the cows down, he thought, and wondered if Pinkey would trail them to the ranch.

There was a noise in the kitchen. Bobby Korematsu, who had come to cook at the ranch twenty years before when McKay was seven, stuffed the woodbox of the cookstove with split pine and lit match after match until a fire roared. He set a bucket of water on the stove to boil, clacking across the floor in *getas* (Japanese clogs) carved the winter before. He wasn't used to cooking for just two. Before the war there had been a full house – the three boys, Pinkey, a haying or calving crew, and irrigators. Bobby had cooked three meals a day for them and no work on the ranch was appreciated more deeply.

14

The first night the ranch was empty after everyone but McKay had gone to the front, McKay found Bobby in the darkened dining room crying. He was sitting on a chair whose legs had been cut down so his feet would reach the floor.

"I don't like fight. Not good for heart," he said, pounding his chest with his small hand. "See, it make me cry."

McKay pulled the elegant chair that had been his mother's so close to Bobby their knees touched but could think of nothing to say. He had lied to Bobby about his brothers, saying they were fighting in Italy when, in fact, they were in the Pacific, because after Pearl Harbor, Bobby had said, "Not possible." Another time Bobby had seen something in the cookstove fire: his Japanese nephews slicing through the bodies of the ranch boys with swords. That night he had stood at McKay's bedroom door and said, "So ashamed," then turned quickly away.

* * *

Pinkey stood at the back of the bar called the Cactus after the owner's mule who liked beer. His bloodied lips moved as he read the new sign stuck in the corner of the mirror behind the bottles. It read: No Japs. He ordered a beer and a shot then his eyes went to the sign again. He gulped the whiskey down, then turned his back on the barman who wanted to talk. Near the door there was a pile of junk on the floor: a 410 shotgun with a broken stock, three rolls of rusted barbed wire, and a stack of bald tires.

"What's this, your dowry?" he asked the woman sitting alone at one of the booths.

"That's Jimmy Luster's stuff. Backed his wagon to the door last night and just started auctioneering things off. Said his old lady quit him so he was going to travel light for awhile."

A man wearing a red neckscarf and a hat with sweat-stains circling the browband clasped an arm around Pinkey's neck.

"You should've got in on that one, Pink. Hell, he would've sold you his wife," he said and laughed hoarsely.

"I bought the cigarette lighter out of his truck. Then some asshole told me he never owned one in his life," a quavering voice said from another booth. Then the speaker held the lighter gleefully in the air.

Pinkey stared at the goods on the floor. "Did Jimmy say where he was headed?"

"Didn't know," the old cowboy with the red scarf said. "See, the thing is, he just found out his kid was killed in the Pacific. Them Japs sank his ship and he was in some kinda lifeboat deal and he went plumb nuts. Jumped overboard. He couldn't swim."

16

Pinkey looked out the front windows of the bar. The bright morning light hurt his eyes. Fat flakes of snow were falling fast. "He'll just winterkill out there," he muttered as if talking about himself. Then he drank for the rest of the day.

* * *

The dogs dug down through five inches of new snow until they reached dirt and lay in their cone-beds with their backs to the wind. McKay brought the horses in and saddled one of them. He had decided to open the pasture gates to let the cattle, who could not paw through snow to eat, drift in. "Open gates, cut wire, do whatever you have to during a blizzard or the cattle will walk into a draw and suffocate there," his father had always warned him.

As he rode, Heart Mountain disappeared from sight. The cloud that took it did so quickly, like a hunger, McKay thought. Now the peak broke the skin of the cloud. Nothing about it resembled a heart. It was, instead, a broken horn or a Cubist breast, as McKay's mother had once remarked. Behind it the Beartooth Mountains veered north. Forty million years ago Heart Mountain broke off from the Rockies and skidded twenty-five miles on a detachment fault to its present site. There was no other limestone in the area like it and at its base was one of the most fertile hayfields on the ranch.

As McKay rode under the limestone tusk he looked up. A half moon hooked its side. So that's how love works, he thought and chuckled out loud. He reduced his mother's geology lesson to a list of words: detachment, skidding, breast, horn, heart. As he said the words a bank of snowclouds took over every mountain west of the ranch, and McKay kicked his horse into a lope. When he reached the first gate, the cattle were already waiting.

*　*　*

Pinkey found his dentures on the sidewalk between the Cactus and the Silver Spur Bars and lost them a third time. He couldn't walk straight. The tremor which began in his neck passed all the way down to his fingertips. A pickup full of young cowboys passed.

"Come on up to the Outlaw and we'll buy you a drink," one of the young men yelled.

A sheet of slush sprayed Pinkey's bowed legs. He looked up. A face in the cab gave him a start. It was his son. Pinkey dove into an alley. He felt sick. His empty stomach convulsed.

"Dad?"

Pinkey leaned between the brick walls of two buildings. "I thought you was up to the Outlaw," he said, trying to straighten up. He had wanted to see his son. He always wanted to see him, it was a hunger like the tug of a good woman in town, but stronger. He remembered he had promised his son he would take the cure.

"I came back to say hi. You in town for a couple of days?" the boy asked.

"You could say that," Pinkey replied dryly. "Oh Christ, I'm going to be sick, you better go."

The dry heaves scratched up through Pinkey's body and ended in his open mouth. He gasped and spit. Vincent held his father's head until the nausea passed.

Pinkey looked at his son. "How'd you get so growed up?"

The young man shrugged shyly but the wounded look in his eyes was there. Pinkey knew the look and concluded he needed one more drink before he quit. They went in. Vincent's broad face bore the scars of acne and from under his tall-crowned black hat two braids hung down. Pinkey ordered two beers.

"Who's your friend?" the bartender asked.

"This is my kid, Vincent," Pinkey replied proudly.

"The hell . . ."

"His mother's Crow. You can tell because he's so tall and good-looking."

"Yeah, but who's the father?" one of the drunks yelled

from the back of the bar. The chirp in his voice sounded more like choking.

"Well I've never seen a half-breed looks like that," the bartender commented.

"That's because you've never been more than two feet out of this sonofabitchin' Mormon town," Pinkey said. He stared at the bartender, who busied himself wiping glasses. Pinkey stood on his toes and leaned toward the man. "We're all half-breeds," he said. "The whole god-damned country is breeds. And what the hell difference does it make? Anyone of you show me some thorough-bred blood and I'll show you a phony sonofabitch."

Pinkey stepped back from the bar. He threw a silver dollar on the counter, turned, kicked the jukebox until it lit up and played a tune, then followed Vincent to the street.

"Hey, Pinkey, do you want your change or is this my tip?" the barman asked.

When Pinkey reached the sidewalk he slipped on the ice. Vincent helped him to his feet.

"I'd better catch that ride to the ranch," Vincent mumbled. "Do you have wheels?"

"Yea. Sure," Pinkey said. The color had drained from his face again. He watched Vincent walk east along the main street. The boy moved like a wildcat, Pinkey thought. Smooth and swift and awake. Maybe he wasn't the kid's father, he thought. He brushed snow from his coat, adjusted his gray Stetson, and looked the opposite way, towards his cattle range, and walked in that direction. Stores gave way to small frame and brick houses where singed lawns burned under the snow. His hat was cocked sideways on his head and he jerked back when a dog barked at him.

Past the last house the sky closed down like a dark awning unreeled from the mountains, lowering what Pinkey thought of as infinity, all the way down to the pint bottle in his back pocket from which he stopped to drink. He wiped his mouth as the liquor slid down. A skunk ran out from behind a rose bush. Pinkey howled with laughter, brushing against the red blossoms skewed with the weight of snow. The skunk zigzagged down the road, the stripe on its back crossing the white line, like crossing his t's, Pinkey thought, and so came to assume that the highway would spell out messages for him if he walked far enough along its edge.

Two dogs came out from behind the Mormon church and trotted at Pinkey's heels. Pinkey turned and whistled to them. For twelve years he had trained the stockdogs at McKay's ranch never addressing them in a voice louder than a whisper. He felt good. He'd wanted company and now he had dogs. He looked at the sky. The clouds had curdled and thickened. He thought of the storm as the product of the penis cloud he'd seen the day before. It had knocked up some old gal and now there was this.

From a distance a red and white graintruck approached the trio. The dogs sprinted ahead, leaping up and changing directions midair to chase the truck. Pinkey watched them. Another truck followed and the dogs repeated their act. Pinkey crouched down and followed the action with his head. He thought he'd give it a try. When the third truck came he ran alongside it and barked. After ten yards he stopped and stood up, puffing, while the dogs jumped up and down in delight. For a long time there were no other vehicles on the road. The trio waited. Wind blew snow into Pinkey's face so he and the dogs clambered down into the borrow pit. Like swimmers, they waded through tall grass, their feet rolling over the tops of beer bottles as they walked.

A car appeared. Pinkey crawled up to the road, clutching bunchgrass as he climbed. The headlights bore down on him. "You jacklightin' sonofabitch," he yelled. The lights were on him like crossed eyes. He didn't know where to look. He crouched down, barking in unison with the dogs, a magnificent high-pitched crooning cut off suddenly by a *whomp*. The car shuddered, fishtailed and slid to a stop. A cyclone fence on the far side of the borrow pit vibrated. Pinkey sprawled against the fence and moaned. The driver of the car ran to the collapsed figure.

"God almighty, mister . . . are you . . ."

Pinkey looked up. The man crouching over him had dark eyes. Like Vincent's. Was this Vincent? No. Then Pinkey remembered why he had come to town that day. It was Vincent's birthday.

"You killed me, you sonofabitch," Pinkey said.

The driver dropped to his knees and began sobbing.

"Well hell, I ain't really dead," Pinkey said and grinned.

The driver wiped his nose.

"Don't just stare at me. Take me to the hospital. I think my leg's busted."

The man pulled off his jacket and spread it across Pinkey's chest. "I'm sorry, man. I'm really sorry."

"Oh shutup," Pinkey said and when he spoke his toothless gums caught the glint of headlights from an oncoming truck.

* * *

McKay drew out a deck of cards thrown loosely in a drawer with the silverware. He had lost seventy-nine games of gin rummy to Bobby in the year 1942 and expected to lose this one. Bobby pushed the worn scorecard across the oilcloth while McKay shuffled and dealt. A truck pulled into the yard. McKay looked at his hand quickly while pushing his chair back to stand up.

"Good god. If this ain't a cobbled up mess. How am I ever going to win a game?"

"Just clean up mess," Bobby said wryly.

Madeleine stood in the doorway. Snow blew into the room and for a moment McKay was mesmerized by the way it hit the tip of her nose and dissolved on her cheeks.

"Pinkey's dead," she said flatly.

"You can't kill that sonofabitch," McKay said. Then a look of alarm came over his face. "Are you sure?"

"No. But you better go to the hospital. That's where they were taking him."

McKay touched Madeleine's shoulder and was gone.

Two women rolled Pinkey into the x-ray room on a gurney. He lay back, his hands folded behind his head.

"Do you want to take my pants off now or later?" he asked the two nurses and winked. They smiled and said nothing.

The transfer to the examining table proceeded with difficulty. Pinkey refused to help. On the contrary, he relaxed further, a deadweight for the two women. McKay burst in. With one motion he lifted his hired hand to the table.

"For god's sake, Pinkey . . ."

Pinkey gave McKay a grin. "Where's the cards, the flowers, the candy?"

Pinkey turned to the nurses. "Are you going to strip me now?" he asked.

"Sorry old man. Maybe another time," the heavier of the two replied. Then she split the seam of his trousers with a razor.

"Stop it! My new pants!" Pinkey howled.

"Just slap the sonofabitch," McKay said and motioned to the nurse to continue cutting.

*   *   *

The hospital let Pinkey sleep it off in the vacant labor room for no extra charge. He slept until the pain in his leg woke him. When he opened his eyes the walls of the room folded down around him and spun. He closed them again. The beads of darkness under his lids spun too, zooming backward then bursting against some inner wall, the color of garnets. He felt a terrible weight in his body. Maybe they put a body cast on with my arms inside so I can't hold a bottle, he thought. He tried to move his arms and swung himself into the black room until he hit something and there was a crash. Then the sickly weight pulled him down.

A switch clicked and the room filled with light like a lung.

"Did we fall out of bed?" a big woman in white asked. She helped Pinkey up.

"I guess my wings broke," he said.

"Up we go. Now, we'll put these sides up so we don't try to fly again."

Pinkey felt the hard bed under him again. When the nurse's face came close he thought he heard a terrible roar like snow falling from a roof. Then the room was black again. He tried to lie still, but his shoulders twitched and his whole body splintered like rotten wood. He saw a bottle somewhere in front of him and when he reached for it, it broke, but the whiskey wouldn't spill. It stood up as if frozen, then all at once, shattered. His arms lengthened, reaching for it. He tried to think of why the need came on him. Then his arms were fifty yards long, his hands like tiny knobs and still he could touch nothing and the need grew, a malevolent bloom.

* * *

"You havin' a baby or do you want to go home?" McKay asked throwing light into the room.

Pinkey sat up and looked around. "Am I dead?"

"How the hell do I know, I ain't the doctor."

"What time is it?" Pinkey asked.

"Morning. And if we don't get home pretty soon, we'll be snowed in for the winter."

"Sounds good to me," Pinkey said. He felt clear-headed suddenly and slid off the bed, hopping on one leg.

McKay handed him the crutches. "God, if you don't look like a jackrabbit."

*   *   *

A fog swallowed the road ahead of McKay's pickup and mixed with steam off the river. They drove north in the dark. Ahead the sky began to clear.

"What'd you have to go and get drunk for?" McKay asked. He was tired.

"That's why."

"What's why?"

"Because I'm tired of having reasons. Why can't a man just go and do stuff?"

"Well you ain't going to be doing much with that thing on your leg."

From out of the dark a roadsign loomed: WELCOME TO BIG SKY COUNTRY—MONTANA. A horse ran in front of the truck. McKay swerved hard.

"Hey. That's my mare," Pinkey shouted and pointed at the horse, now saddleless, eating what McKay referred to as "government feed" which meant the grass on the side of the highway.

The truck skidded to a halt. Pinkey looked. He could see the blurred outline of the calcium plant. A half moon shot up out of empty railroad cars and stars shone like pinholes in ice. Across the road his saddle had been dumped on end under the bar sign which pulsed throwing a bloody pool on the snow every second or so. Dawn broke as pink and dry as calcium dust. Though Pinkey knew the sight had something to do with how the future becomes the present and the present the future, he still felt like a banty rooster crowing at first light, not caring or knowing what it portended.

McKay backed the pickup to a sidehill and loaded the mare. Pinkey rolled down his window. "I named her Eleanor, for Eleanor Roosevelt," he said.

McKay slapped the horse on the rump and she jumped in. The top of her back steamed where snow had melted and the ice hanging in her mane clanged together like a crystal chandelier.

McKay turned the truck around and they drove south. Now the sign read: WELCOME TO BIG WONDERFUL WYOMING. Pinkey inspected his cast as if seeing it for the first time. He drummed on it here and there and discovered some of the plaster was still wet.

"Don't you worry about them cows," he said. "I left them on auto pilot. And don't worry about this cast either. We'll cut her off in a couple of weeks and I'll be good as new."

A smile came over McKay's face but the old man didn't see it. They drove in silence. Pinkey pulled his coat tightly around him. He cradled his head with a gloved hand and a wheezing snore came from his half-opened mouth and filled the cab with a sound that reminded McKay of peace.

The truck bumped along the ungraded ranch road. McKay stopped once to check a mudhole and when he climbed back in, he looked at the old cowboy with affection. In his sleep, Pinkey felt Mckay's eyes on him. It was like heat penetrating his heavy lids. He wanted to laugh, but his body made no sound.

2

KAI AND BOBBY

HE LAY ACROSS the bed with only a shirt on. It was late and it was raining again. After Li made love to him she rested her head on his stomach.

"You nervous. Everything noisy in there," she said.

Kai shifted, laughing, and pulled one knee up. Then he reached over and lit a cigarette. The room smelled of green vegetables and cooking oil. Li climbed off the bed.

"Here," she said, pinning a badge to Kai's shirt. She kissed his chest. The noise of the city wallowed in the room, a mechanical gargling of horns, rain and engines. On the fire escape the potted chrysanthemum Kai had given to Li on her birthday tossed about in the wind. Kai contemplated the badge. He ground the butt of his cigarette out until it looked like a pig's flared snout, then clasped Li's head tightly in the crook of his arm. Her hair shone like the stalks of black bamboo. He rolled her from side to side, his arms locked across the small of her back, his legs entwined with hers until she wrigggled away from him. He grabbed her again and pinned her down with a wrestler's hold on her neck.

"Hello," he said.

Li smiled. Her small swimmer's kicks knocked against his shins, then she went limp and floated toward him. Kai dropped heavily beside her. A coolness shifted through his body. Li examined his face.

"Who are you?" she said.

* * *

That was a Thursday in September of 1942. Two days later Kai and his parents were on a train. All through the cars he could see only black hair, dark eyes, the sound of a language his parents had forbidden him to learn. The journal he began keeping tht day ws a way of steadying himself against drastic change. The lullaby rocking on train tracks felt deathly to him. He dreamed the tracks were his arms. He was holding Li. The heavy cars rolled over them.

When Kai woke his arms were asleep. He had been sitting on his hands. Out the train window the desert looked like the palm of a hand on which life had drawn no lines.

In San Francisco Jimmy Wong, Li's older brother by twelve years, had burst into their room.

"No more Chinese women for you," he'd said and

winked at Kai. He handed Kai a final edition of the *hronicle*. It read: ALL JAPS MUST GO!

Jimmy turned solemn. He plunked down on the bed and looked out the window. The building across the street that housed the dumpling shop and the mahjong room was dark. A fire escape hung tentatively to its side and a green dragon, used in the New Year's parade, lay unfurled against three upstairs windows.

Jimmy whispered: "You stay here. Marry Li. Keep going to college. Change from great Japanese scholar to great Chinaman."

As he spoke the rain intensified and enclosed the streets of Chinatown like sea lanes in a fog that led to places no one in that room knew.

Kai unpinned the badge and twirled it between his fingers. The safety pin pricked his thumb. A drop of blood appeared. Li held his thumb up and licked the blood away. Kai would remember her diminutiveness, standing naked in that noisy room, he would remember the tart taste of her skin.

He pulled his hand away from her and flung it over his head in a mocking backstroke as if to swim from intimacy. She opened the window. Cold rain blew in. She pulled the potted plant whose heavy white blossoms were bent completely over into the room.

* * *

33

Like a great elastic band the train stretched Kai away from that magnetic point on the compass. In his journal he wrote:

> Slowly the train steamed out of Berkeley. As I looked out the window I could see the green hills dotted with houses. Strange but I hadn't noticed the soft greenness before. I remembered that in the hurried retreat I had left my room in turmoil. An Issei would have been ashamed to leave the place in less than perfect order so as not to betray any confusion in his mind.

That last night Kai had waited for sunrise in an all-night upstairs tea shop. There was a curfew for "all people of Japanese ancestry" and it would have been dangerous for him to walk the streets after dark. At nine he boarded the ferry to Richmond. He hadn't seen his parents for two years. The man at the ticket office, a Filipino, had hesitated before giving Kai passage.

"He didn't say anything. He just looked at me and held onto that stub," Kai told his father after their strained, awkward greeting. Later, alone in the kitchen with his mother, she told Kai that his father hadn't recognized him at first.

"Can you imagine?" she said. Then, "He's getting more and more like that."

In the living room Mr. Nagouchi bent toward the big

radio. It lit his face like a jack o'lantern. Kai's mother stirred scallions into broth, shoyu, and sake, then eggs and eel.

"I don't eat this food very often anymore," Kai said.

"Oh, this is special for you. *Unagi donburi*. You always liked it," she said, though Kai could remember liking no such thing.

After lunch Kai and his father drove to town. Mr. Nagouchi wanted to show his son the store.

Mr. Nagouchi grunted, "No good now." It was Wednesday but Japantown was deserted. Mr. Nagouchi unlocked the door. It was a triangular building at the end of a block flanked by two narrow streets. When Kai walked up and down the aisles, the floorboards squeaked. He looked at shelves of tools—planers, chisels, Japanese saws, and a ceiling-high stack of black twine rolled into balls. In another aisle were rice cookers, bamboo water ladles, brass teapots, packets of seed, and a penny jar full of bubble gum.

Mr. Nagouchi took his place behind the counter for the last time. Behind his head was the business license he'd framed austerely in black and next to it, a photograph of the great Buddha at Nara.

"For god's sake, Pop, take that down. Have Mom bring the Navy pictures or something," Kai said.

Mr. Nagouchi stood motionless. The son he had sent away to be raised as a scholar was giving him orders the way American boys did. Kai inserted a penny into the jar and popped a jaw-breaker into his mouth. When his father struggled with a lock at the back door, Kai helped him. Finally the door swung open. Instead of the street, there was a garden — a tiny miniaturized place with stepping stones, mossy banks, a stone water basin, three flowering shrubs, and against a tall fence, a thicket of black bamboo.

"I sold the business yesterday," Kai's father said solemnly. "Seven hundred. The car too. But I didn't show them this."

Kai spit his gum into his hand and stared at the massive block of stone under his feet. Already the moss had begun to grow beyond its borders. Across the street a bell in the Buddhist temple rang. Then Kai heard glass breaking. He looked around. Mr. Nagouchi had broken the picture frame and held a match to the photograph of the Buddha at Nara. The glossy paper lifted and curled toward the old man and became ash.

They locked the store and got in the Studebaker. Sometimes the horn stuck and Mr. Nagouchi had to lift the hood and pinch a certain wire, but not today. They glided through empty streets. Their first night of evacuation would be spent at a racetrack in converted horse-stalls. The idea amused Kai at first, and he thought of bringing a rake from the store for the manure, but changed his mind.

"Seabiscuit, here we come," he said, though quietly so his father would not hear.

*   *   *

The train lurched to a stop. There was no town. Only a water tank and a switchbox. Kai closed his journal and ran to the train door. He jumped down to the wooden platform, tilted his head back and inhaled dry air deeply. Two army soldiers eyed him. They had guns. Steam from the train's engine hissed and the great trunk that was the water hose swung against the black cab. Ahead Kai could see the Rocky Mountains. Snow covered the higher peaks. "Bring clothes suited to pioneer life," they had been advised. The thought had made Kai chuckle.

A handsome couple joined Kai on the platform. They introduced themselves as Will Okubo and Mariko Abe. They had been living in Paris. She was a painter. Kai didn't catch what Will Okubo said about himself. He was tall, lean and pale and used a cigarette holder. His khaki pants were held up by suspenders and he sported a white beret. Some pioneer, Kai thought. Mariko's hair looked like a raven's wing. She pursed her lips when she listened and fastened her wild eyes on one thing, then another, as if to keep the fragments whole in her mind.

An "all aboard" sounded. The trio put out their cigarettes and climbed on the train. In the aisle they nodded to one another and parted. Kai looked in on his parents. The had slept through the stop. His mother's mouth was open and his father's head was tucked against his shoulder the way a bird sleeps and his glasses hung crookedly from his nose. Kai began a letter:

Dear Li,

Can you imagine how I feel? I don't even know myself. A little while ago a wave of loneliness came over me like nothing I've felt before. Then I met two interesting people at a stop in the middle of nowhere. In fact, I don't know where we are. They could be taking us to hell, for all I know. So I keep trying to think of this ridiculous lapse in the democratic process as an adventure. Maybe that's just being naive.

Tell Jimmy we've been following a river called the Virgin River all afternoon, and it runs red. Can you beat that? Otherwise, it's awfully desolate out here. When we left the Assembly Center I saw a man with his arms stuck through a fence, holding his girlfriend, and it made me think of you. But for the time being, I'm a family man. Isn't that funny after all those years as an orphan? Mom and Pop are awfully scared and sad. I've been trying to make the trip comfortable for them but it's hard. Some of this American food they've been eating has made them sick. They'd never had a hamburger before. After all those years in Richmond. By the way, I told them about you.

Pop has hardly said a word since he closed up the store. It's heartbreaking. I can't believe I won't be going to school again for a long time and, in the evenings, coming to you.

We heard that at another camp someone sent a box of oranges with a sword inside. A Nisei ran with it and the MP's shot him dead. They must be taking lessons from Hitler.

I guess I'll try to get some sleep now. I feel so strange being apart from you. It's like I have a big hole in my back that grows bigger and bigger where my heart has flown out and travels towards you.

love, Kai

He closed his journal and slept. Not long afterward and still in the dark, the train, with its five hundred bewildered passengers, reached Heart Mountain Relocation Camp, a cluster of buildings on a barren plain surrounded by mountains and low hills.

After several hours of confusion the families found their way to the barracks and began to settle in. Kai and his parents were assigned an apartment next door to Mariko, Will Okubo, and Mr. Abe. At first Kai's father sat on his suitcase and could not be moved. Then he started crying. Finally Kai and Will lifted the old man to his feet and escorted him to his new home.

Afterward the two young men had a smoke outside. The tar-papered barracks behind them shuddered each time the wind gusted. First light came, then the sun rode the sidehills and sage-covered bench above them. They saw a little bunch of antelope and a family of deer. Already the grass had turned fawn-colored, and the does and fawns had begun to turn dark. A coyote threaded his way along a fenceline towards Heart Mountain. Its long fur was silver.

Will's cigarette burned quickly to the edge of its ivory holder. He was shivering. Kai looked at him, then gave him his jacket. On the ridge above the Camp a line of cattle filed by. A blackbird rode the back of one bull and a lone rider brought up the rear of the procession.

"Do you think he sees us?" Will asked.

Kai shrugged and strained to decipher the face of the man, who soon rode out of sight. When the sun reached the Camp it threw a grillwork of fence shadows across Will and Kai and the shadows of the guard towers leaned sideways, penetrating the barracks and moving across the beds of those who dove fitfully into sleep.

"Tres formidable, huh?" Will said.

Kai threw his cigarette on the dry ground.

"God, there's nothing here," he said and smiled incredulously.

* * *

The handrail over the footbridge to Bobby's cabin was made of barbed wire. Each evening when the footing was slick from dew or ice he steadied himself on it the way he had held the ship's railing when he made the crossing to America forty-five years ago. He had cut his hands on the wire only twice: once, when he heard McKay's sobs of grief on hearing his parents were dead, and again, the night the electricity for the hastily constructed relocation camp was turned on and the southern horizon of the ranch was struck with light.

Bobby had heard the trains pulling in since August. He was not used to noises on the ranch other than the ones made by weaned calves or haying machines or meadowlarks. Too far away to pick out distinct human voices, there was only a low roar that would increase in volume as the camp grew to 10,000 souls and Bobby would remark that it was the biggest city he had seen since leaving his parents' kimono store near the crowded wharfs of Osaka.

When Bobby lit the cookstove that September morning a wasp, still comatose from last night's hard frost, burned to a crisp on the back lid. Pinkey, the only hired hand left on the ranch since the war began, ate the breakfast Bobby made for him. A purple bruise had flowered on his left cheek since the accident and he was having trouble negotiating his way on crutches. All the time he mouthed his pancakes, Bobby thought about wasps and snow. They were part of a long seasonal progression linked and curving through time like the deer spine he had found draped gracefully on a rock outside his cabin door. Rain, flies and mud swallows were followed by heat, mosquitoes, and deerflies, followed by rainlessness, grasshoppers and rattlesnakes, then, as a last gasp before the glittering apocalypse of winter, wasps and the first snows.

Of Osaka Bobby remembered little. Only interminable rain, wharf rats and the bright foliage of kimonos above his bed: Colors like green winter melons and pale chrysanthemum half lost in dark silk folds.

Four buckets of water came to a boil on the cookstove. Bobby poured them into a big galvanized tub on the floor. Naked except for the cast which ended just below the knee and which he referred to as "that half-mast sonofabitch," Pinkey looked round and cherubic and insisted on bathing with his hat on. Bobby tested the water with his little finger.

"Hey, this ain't baby formula we're cookin' up is it?"

Bobby shook his head.

"How the hell do I get in?"

Bobby offered his shoulder. With a great, awkward effort Pinkey lunged over the side of the tub with his broken leg airborne and eased himself into the water. Then, with a magician's flourish, he pulled a packet of bubble bath from under his hat and poured it in.

In Osaka there had been the baths—dark, echoing, humid places with tile floors and the rubbery bodies of sailors and working men. Bobby thought about the uniformed men who had come to the ranch the week before. McKay, who was on horseback, stopped them before they reached the house. The one man had a crewcut, a cactus stand of hair, and the other had long fingers that turned up at the end like those of wealthy men who hane never dug a posthole or roped a calf. McKay had sat his horse stiffly and when the strangers got back into their Army car he had pulled his hat down and wheeled the horse to the barn.

There had been another visitor that night. McKay had found Madeleine sitting on the steps on the screened porch. Her head was in her arms and snow was collecting in the brim of her hat. She had received a telegram. Her husband, Henry, had been taken prisoner of war, not in Germany as Bobby had been told, but in Japan. Later she and McKay came into the kitchen.

"What will they do to him?" she had asked Bobby, who, instead of replying, fled the room.

Pinkey hummed as he washed behind his ears. He let his hands float on top of the water and gathered bubbles toward his chest until he had amassed two prodigious breasts. When they dissolved Bobby helped him out of the tub. Pinkey hopped to a chair and began to dry himself—face, neck, under his arms, his legs and balls. When he looked up he found Bobby staring at him.

"You think I bad now? Should go to Camp with other Japanese?" Bobby asked.

Pinkey stopped dabbing. He felt uneasy. A sadness came forward from somewhere behind or below the optic nerve in his eye and poured itself around the black iris until the whole face softened. Finally Pinkey spoke.

"You and I've been on this outfit a long time and I figure we're just about the same man. We both come away from home when we was kids and we know how to live high on the hog and how to survive too. And we know what makes people tick because they ain't no different than the coyotes or that horse herd out there and we damn sure have to get along with them to survive. And we're both gettin' old. And under this is just an ol' boneyard, ain't it? Just a bunch of bones and once they're scattered on the ground who will know which is mine and which is yours and which is the coyotes?"

Bobby let his small body down on the chair. His feet swung under him because they did not touch the floor. Then he looked at Pinkey and dug into his pocket and pulled carefully folded news clippings out and gave them to the old cowboy. Pinkey handed them back.

"You read them. I ain't got my glasses on."

Bobby read: " 'PARK COUNTY SAYS NO TO JAPS HERE' 'A JAP IS A JAP' ".

Pinkey sat motionless in the chair. Bath water had dripped around his feet. Then he held up one of his crutches and swung it like a baseball bat as though fighting off invisible demons in the air.

Bobby finished the ranch chores early. Pinkey had fallen asleep by the fire and Bobby was careful not to wake him. In the hallway he pulled on his boots then bundled up in a wool coat. He left the house by the kitchen door and walked south accompanied by two Red Heelers who would not stay home. Once, where the road became the creek and the creek the road, Bobby thought about how easily one thing can become another, how chameleon and insubstantial we are. By mid-afternoon he had reached the Heart Mountain Camp.

* * *

Three young Nisei boys goose stepped by the guardhouse and saluted. "Heil, Hitler," they boomed out, then broke into a run. Momentarily distracted, the MP's let Bobby through the gate. The two red dogs stayed on the other side of the fence and whined.

Bobby walked past rows and rows of block housing. At the end of each building men and women picked through scraps of lumber. From the shower rooms a tall

45

woman in a silk robe ran along a muddy walkway. Her wet hair had turned white with frost. A baby cried. Plumes of smoke churned from each building and merged with snowclouds. When he thought he might meet someone he knew, some member of his family perhaps, his heart drummed and his pulse felt ropey and he imagined the blood running through him as yellow sap. He walked and walked like an insomniac.

As evening came on he could see into the living quarters. The woman he had seen in the silk robe tousled her hair in front of a wood stove. An emaciated young man lay on a bed behind her. He blew smoke rings in the air and spoke French, not English or Japanese. Through another window Bobby saw an old man crying into a white handkerchief, three teenage girls giggling over a magazine, and a young man standing at the window writing in a journal and smoking. Then he came on three old men hunched over a Go board. They spoke to one another in Japanese. Bobby listened. He gargled the familiar words in his mouth. The sounds hit the back of his teeth, but they no longer carried any meaning. Bobby was shocked to find he had forgotten so much. The words fluttered, landing nowhere. But he remembered Go, and the snap of white and black stones on wood went off inside him like switches.

It was dark. Bobby's dogs lay curled against each other at the sentry gate. A half moon came and went behind clouds and Heart Mountain brightened and darkened accordingly. An MP with a Coke in his hand came to the guardhouse door.

"Pass please."

"No live here . . . I'm cook for twenty years at Heart Ranch," Bobby said and pointed upcountry.

The MP turned to his partner. "We have another joker out here."

"What's your name, boy?"

"I'm not boy. Old enough to be your grandfather."

The soldiers laughed. On the hill behind them a family of coyotes began yipping. Bobby's dogs growled and went after them. When Bobby tried to call them back, they wouldn't come.

"Who are you then?" the soldier asked.

Bobby gave his name. He looked in the direction of the ranch but could see no lights. The Big Dipper bent its elbow down where the ranch should have been. He thought of the trains he had seen coming in, full of Nisei and Issei, the "yellow peril," and how those trains travelled on track he had helped build, and how they were bringing everything he had forgotten he was back to him.

The soldiers motioned Bobby into the guardhouse. They had been playing checkers. Bobby sat down and folded his hands. The coyotes had stopped howling and it was quiet. A terrible, raw quiet. Then a voice said Bobby's name. He stood up and went to the door and a short, ruddy man wearing a gray Stetson cocked sideways on his head and propelling himself forward on crutches appeared.

3.

McKAY

"The weather spirit is blowing the storm out, the weather spirit is driving the weeping snow away over the earth, and the helpless storm-child Narsuk shakes the lungs of the air with his weeping."

COOPER ESKIMO

WHEN MCKAY WOKE there was a dead rooster on the floor. He sat up with a start because he was in the wrong bedroom. He picked up the bird. At first he didn't know how it had landed there, then he remembered the cockfight the night before. The rooster was light in his hands. Its scarlet comb had been clipped short and at the back of each yellow foot a sharpened spur protruded, white as a woman's fingernail.

McKay stood and the room went black. There was no heat in that part of the house, and he pulled on his long underwear quickly. As he straightened the bed he caught sight of himself in the mirror: one side of his face looked old, the eye twitched and the soft flesh under the eye was gray as if ash had been smeared there; the other side, the bright side, looked childlike, the way one corner of the mouth was pulled down, and the split face was topped by one insouciant tumble of blond hair.

He called for Bobby, the cook, but no one answered. It was the third day of a savage, unseasonal storm. During the night a cloud shaped like an appendix had burst, dropping its white cargo like poison, and wind had violated the one tree. Its green topknot had exploded and dropped branches into the arms of lower limbs like bodies being carried home from war.

The house had never seemed so quiet. When McKay looked down into the living room from the balcony, he saw that everything was covered with snow. In front of each window and door were dunecaps of white. Some had toppled sideways. Wind had sprayed snow over furniture, into the black corners of the fireplace and across the Navajo rugs on the floor.

McKay hobbled down the stairs. Today was the thirteenth anniversary of his parents' death. They had drowned when their car rolled into an irrigation canal. He picked up their silver-framed photograph taken the day they died. His mother was bundled in a fur coat. Her gray eyes sparkled, and she was smiling at McKay's father whose black hair stood on end. It had been windy. He had the hurt, far-off look of someone who only found happiness elsewhere.

McKay went to the kitchen and stoked the cookstove. Outside, wind had swept the ground almost free of snow. Only the buildings and fencelines were drifted. He pulled a stool up and turned the radio on. Each morning McKay braced himself for bad news, expecting to hear his brothers' names on the casualty list. Instead, there was no news at all.

After his brothers left to go to war the rooms of the house felt too big and the huge pasture McKay rode to check cows looked like the moon. The sky went gray as if the planet had turned from the sun, averting its face. Sometimes McKay imagined one of the bombs had gone astray and floated alongside him. His loneliness took on a metallic glare—metal flying fast. The snowdrifts at the doors pressed at him and the ungodly stillness roared.

* * *

The morning of the cockfight McKay rode out through the west gate towards a sheepcamp where he was to meet his neighbor, Madeleine. It was shipping day. The ranchers had gathered their cattle and trailed them to sorting corrals where they would be shipped by rail to Omaha. On the way McKay saw seven cow elk on the flank of Heart Mountain. A young bull bugled, his low whistle ascending sharply until air caught at the entrance to his throat, then he gave out three seal-like grunting cries. The bull approached a cow. He thrust a knee between her back legs and horned her, tilting his branching antlers into her rump. She jumped and ran. He pursued her, lifting his nose in the air to inhale the full brunt of her sexual fragrance.

McKay dropped down the slope to a creekbed and entered a canyon. It narrowed quickly. The straight-up red walls hemmed him in. Far above, thin pine trees swan-necked out from cracks in the rock, then grew straight towards the sky. Occasionally, three-foot long icicles dropped, taking the air like harpoons. One arced past the horse's nose then broke like crystal stemware across the trail. McKay watched the tracks in front of his horse: deer, elk, rabbit, bird and bobcat. They looked like music to him, a skating, hopping, notational scrawl left behind by players who had gone elsewhere.

At the far end the canyon widened and McKay rode to Raoul's camp. Madeleine wasn't there. He warmed himself by the tiny cookstove inside the wagon. On the bed was a Bible and a loaded rifle. He remembered the night he and Raoul had been snowed in together. They had shared the high built-in bed across the back of the wagon. The old sheepherder had lit a candle and their shadows blossomed on the rounded ceiling. That was the night he told McKay about the hurricane.

"The *tomenta*—that is what we called the hurricane in Mexico. She comes on so fast, see . . . sand blowing so hard I can't see nothing. Then it grows dark, and it rains. Our village is on a hill, and all of us are crowding together praying. We hear a big roar, like God himself talking, and we run out to see what has happened. It is the hill falling. It is water running everywhere. The woman, she is standing next to me, holding her baby. The water comes and sweeps that baby right out of her arms . . . then she goes too. Just like that — all that creation — pufff. Then I *knew* it was God talking. In the morning I see the whole village is gone. Well then, what am I to do? So I walk all the way to La Paz. Three days I am walking. When I get there I meet others just like me — who have come from nothing, who have nothing. But pretty soon we find jobs. And the man whose wife was washed away, he meets another woman and starts his life all over again. In no time he is happy. You think is crazy? But life is like that. *La vida es muy historica, no?*"

Then Raoul blew out the candle and McKay rolled onto his side, away from the old man, and pretended to sleep.

*   *   *

McKay rode on following two sets of horsetracks across a ridge, down into a coulee. Two eagles circled. He saw Madeleine and Raoul digging sheep out of a snowdrift that had curled back at the top like an upper lip sneering. McKay stepped off his horse.

"I guess they just gave up and suffocated," Madeleine said, handing McKay the back legs of two bloated ewes. When they dragged the last of seven dead sheep from the drift it collapsed into a white ruin like the cities of Europe that had been destroyed.

Raoul emerged from the timber with five crosses made from pine twigs tied at the center with bits of string. He kneeled in front of the dead sheep and planted the crosses in the snow.

Afterward Madeleine and McKay rode towards town. They had been childhood friends, then lovers. By the time she surrendered her virginity to him and his to her in a dry irrigation ditch wrapped in a canvas dam that smelled of mildew, they had already worked cattle, roped, and ridden colts together and continued to do so. They had been born on the same day in the same hospital, McKay in the delivery room and Madeleine in the labor room, there being only one of each in the small country hospital, and when she came home after four years of college with a husband on her arm McKay felt as welcoming to the man as he did betrayed.

They rode for a time without talking. McKay liked the way she sat a horse: she took a deep seat and kept a light hand. A fresh set of clouds billowed and leapfrogged across the face of Heart Mountain. They stopped for lunch though McKay wasn't hungry. He'd finally understood the arbitrariness of life since the War had begun: it was vicarious shellshock—black dreams, trembling, an absence of the small lusts.

He unrolled his yellow slicker and laid it across an outcropping of rock. From their perch he and Madeleine could see a corner of the Relocation Camp. McKay uncorked his flask and offered it to Madeleine. She took a swallow and wiped her mouth. It had been a week since she had heard her husband, Henry, had been taken prisoner of war in Japan.

McKay unwrapped a sandwich for her. She watched as he fed his to his dog.

"What are you thinking about?" she asked. She always asked the questions she wanted someone to ask her.

"Henry," McKay said.

"Are you thinking well of him?"

"That's a mean thing to say," McKay said and looked at her.

"Maybe he's dead, anyway," she said bitterly.

Down at the Camp they heard roosters crowing and the lines of a baseball diamond showed through melting snow. McKay leaned back on the rock and closed his eyes.

"Are you sure you want to ride to Omaha with the cattle?" he asked sleepily.

"Are you worried about me?"

"Hell no. It just means I'll be short-handed for a week."

"Thanks," she said and mussed his hair playfully. He looked at her. The gray light made her eyes turn violet.

"I'll miss you," she said almost inaudibly.

He turned toward her. Under the hat her long hair was tucked behind an ear whose convolutions shone, inviting him to fall in there. A tumbling rock startled them. McKay smiled his crooked, mischievous smile.

"I think you were the first person I saw when I was born," he said.

* * *

The shipping corrals loomed against the sky, and everywhere there was great commotion. Weaned calves bawled for their mothers, yardmen snapped bullwhips over the backs of steers, cowboys on horseback pushed a penful of heifers down a wide alley to a loading chute. Waiting boxcars thumped forward as each was loaded.

For the rest of the day McKay and Madeleine worked the chute. They pushed steers up the slippery ramp, sometimes hoisting them bodily. Some fell and had to be righted, others turned so they were facing backward in the chute. Madeleine and McKay were kicked and tromped, their pantlegs green with manure. Falling snow piled up in their hatbrims as they worked.

When the door of the last cattle car rolled shut, Madeleine unsaddled her horse and let him drink and roll in an empty pen. The window of the cafe across the road had steamed up and the lights looked like an ornament against so much desolate land. She grabbed McKay's arm and drew him toward her. Just then the yardlights came on and shadows from the sorting corrals made bars across her face.

McKay remembered the night the telegram about Henry had come. He had urged Madeleine to stay the night at the ranch. Bobby had made a bed in an upstairs room and led her the length of the balcony with a kerosene lamp. Once again their twin lives were stacked like a double entendre. He had felt her presence in the house that night as some kind of tenderness swelling. It filled him and somehow he was lifted up through the ceiling to her bed.

Now her teeth chattered. Snow blew in a crossfire between them. McKay closed his eyes. It seemed they were naked and he was moving in and out of her like a furred animal, long and warm and sweet, standing on his hind legs. To be inside her he had to hitch his whole body up and when he came or thought he had come, water rushed by the narrow bones in his face, and he heard sheets of ice cracking. Then he was cold as if he had been without clothes all winter. The air was dry. The dryness

57

crackled between them and a spark popped when he finally touched her arm.

Now McKay clasped Madeleine's arm so tightly his knuckles turned white. He didn't know if he was shaking her or if the cold in her body was shaking him, or if, in stopping her embrace he had intended to pull her against him. Her amethyst eyes shone.

"I'm sorry," she said, and the flush on her cheeks travelled sideways to her ears.

* * *

McKay carried his dog into the cafe. It was hot inside and the floor was greasy with melted snow and mud. He swung onto the stool at the long counter. The dog curled up at his feet and began snoring. The room was full with men. Those who weren't eating stood behind those who were, and each time the door swung open the noise inside the cafe redoubled with the sound of bawling calves.

"McKay?" Carol Lyman stood in front of the young rancher, coffee pot suspended in air. He nodded. She poured, then turned, catching a glimpse of herself in the mirror, and primped her brittle hair.

"And I'll have a piece of that pie," McKay said.

She slid a plate toward him.

"And the little shit probably wants a hamburger," he said indicating the dog on the floor.

"With everything?"

"No onions," he said and winked at her.

More bodies crowded in behind McKay, men he had known all his life, men his father's age, bundled in long wool coats and tall boots.

"I'll have a whiskey and ditch of some of that pie," one of them shouted.

"Which kind?"

"I don't care. Just one of them round ones," he said and broke into laughter.

Two old cowboys shouldered in behind McKay and set their cups on the counter to be refilled.

". . . Hell no, I was tied hard and fast and when that ol' bull hit the end of the rope he whipped around . . ."

Carol Lyman returned with the pie.

"Where's my whiskey?" the man asked.

"It's too damned early for you to be starting on that stuff," she said curtly and poured the coffee for the cowboys.

". . . And my horse backed up so fast the saddle rode up on his neck. Hell I was sittin' plumb between his ears . . ."

"Well it's been a crazy goddamned storm. Those guys over in Sheridan really got it bad. Lost forty-five percent of their lamb crop, I heard . . ."

". . . And she went out in the morning and they was just dead cows and horses everywhere. Then her hired man come up froze to death. Christ, things is bad enough with this war going on without a mess like that. Poor woman."

Carol Lyman brought the dog's hamburger and refilled McKay's cup. "No onions."

"No onions," he replied.

One of the yardmen talked to someone behind him. "Hey, did you hear about Fred's boy and Henry? They was taken prisoner of war by them dirty Japs."

"I think I could stand anything but that," a voice behind McKay said.

"Carol, where's my whiskey at?"

"You eat that pie first."

"Well when was you hired on to be my mother?"

Carol snorted and turned on her heel. Steam from the coffee pot flew over her shoulder like a feather boa.

"Shutup everyone . . . excuse me, Ma'm . . . I think the news is coming on," one of the ranchers said.

The seat next to McKay emptied ad filled up again.

"How'd you fare, McKay? Get those onery old cows of your loaded up?"

"Yep. I guess we did."

Carol Lyman removed the empty pie plate from in front of McKay and wiped the counter clean. Her quick movements reminded McKay of his mother. That's how his memory of her worked: nothing whole came to him, just parts of her in motion—a turbulence he could feel as she passed from room to room, a fragrance ballooning out of her.

McKay looked out the window. someone had wiped the panes clean. The sorting pens were full again with another man's cattle and through the slats of the cars he could see the bulge of a rump and protruding horns.

"There goes more Japs," someone yelled excitedly.

A passenger train slid behind the cattle cars on another track. The shades were all drawn.

"I don't see how they could get any more in that camp."

"They say there's going to be ten thousand of them."

"Hell, I ain't even seen that many cattle in one bunch before."

Instead of the news, music came on the radio. An old cowboy with a hat shaped like a volcano and no front teeth grabbed Carol Lyman's hand and tugged at her until she came out from behind the counter. The crowd made a space for the couple in the center of the cafe and they waltzed.

McKay thought about the day his parents' car had been pulled from the canal. Something across the road had caught his eye: a woman standing in the doorway of the beauty parlor. As she watched the rescue crew, a curler dropped from her head—like an antler, McKay

61

thought—and bounced on the floor. The woman was Carol Lyman.

"I heard Madeleine's gonna ride with them cows," the man next to McKay said.

"Yep. She sure is."

"I wonder what poor old Henry would think of that."

McKay warmed his hands around his coffee cup and said nothing.

The blacksmith took Carol Lyman's place behind the counter and started pouring coffee. He stopped in front of McKay.

"I've been thinking about your Ma and Pa this morning," he said quietly.

"Well thank you, Fred," McKay said.

"I guess you must be having a time out there . . . kinda lonely on that ranch, isn't it? Kinda lonely for a young man . . ."

McKay looked down, then out the window. His face had reddened. When Madeleine entered, every man in the cafe turned to look at her.

* * *

It was dark when the "all aboard" sounded. Snow blew across the tall yardlights like black gravel. Madeleine boarded the train. She wore a long yellow slicker over her chaps, and her hat was pulled down low against the wind.

"Call when you get to Omaha," McKay yelled up to her. "And watch for that shipping fever. I had Bobby pack the medicine kit. And if you need help that kid from the Two Dot Ranch is on board somewhere."

"Yes, McKay," she said and winked.

"And be careful . . ."

The train lurched once and stopped. They could hear cattle scramble for footing, then the train lurched again.

"McKay, I'm sorry."

"For what?"

Madeleine shrugged. Then the train moved and she slid away from him.

* * *

McKay went to the cockfight before going home. He slid down the hill to the gravel wash under the flume. The two old men, Manuel and Tony, were weighing their roosters on an old packer's scale. Then they dropped the birds onto the frozen ground swept clean of rock and lit uncertainly by three hissing Coleman lanterns.

The brown rooster had a speckled neck and red tail feathers. The other had black wings flecked with irides-cent green. Parts of its body had been plucked and the bare skin looked blue. Bronze feathers streamed down the bird's neck. They stood on end when the birds went at each other, forming a ruffled collar.

At first the birds pecked timidly and nuzzled neck to neck — like lovers, McKay thought. Then the brown bird jumped straight up, lashing out with his sharpened spurs as he came down. The black bird ducked, leapt and gashed back. They used their beaks and feet, pecking at each other's heads until blood came. They jumped again, and when they came down this time, the brown rooster's spur stuck into the black bird's neck and blood from the jugular flowed onto the ground.

A bottle of tequila was passed. Manuel dropped to his hands and knees over the dead rooster and when he stood again the front of his shirt was stained red. A man passed the tequila to McKay with a wild grin on his face. McKay raised the bottle in honor of the dead cock and tilted his head back until a line of stars — Orion's belt — rushed through his head. The gold liquid tasted like mineral, and something overripe and very green. When they took the bottle from him he knelt down and stroked the dead rooster. "Bird of paradise," he thought, and imagined the feathers were really a woman's hair. He clutched the bird to his chest, rolled over and smiled.

McKay took the shortcut home in the dark. His horse climbed through the breaks. Snow from juniper branches spilled down his neck as he brushed by. His companion, the errant bomb, made a little wind just above his head. When the horse climbed to the top of the bench McKay could see the train, at a great distance now, shooting in a straight line east across the Basin.

He didn't know how long he rode with his eyes closed. Blasts of snow scratched his face like crushed oyster shells and the electric needle of hard cold punctured each toe. A dead rooster tied with two saddle strings, hung behind his rolled slicker. When he opened his eyes, McKay knew he had reached the lower end of the ranch.

He passed the gate and climbed the knob toward the family graveyard. When he reached the top he stepped off his horse. Snow from the ground blew up in his face, then plummeted mixing with new snow. McKay could see nothing but white. He leaned toward the ground and pawed the air: no gravestone. A noise startled the horse and the reins pulled out of McKay's numb hands.

"Shit." He kicked at snow. His foot hit something hard. He crouched down and brushed snow away but it was a rock, not his parents' headstone. Something—either the tequila or blowing snow—made his eyes close again.

McKay woke with a start and whistled. His dog came to him. He began a blindman's search for his horse. He walked back and forth, circling one way, then the other. He tripped and his hands slid across polished rock.

"Hello, Pa," he said and threw and arm around the gravestone.

"Just this once tell me where my damned horse is, will you?" he said, cupping his hands to the grave. His nose was running and tufts of blond hair stuck out from under his hat. Suddenly he stood and walked toward a tree. A dark form appeared behind the trunk.

"Well you dumb sonofabitch," he said and planted a kiss on the horse's jaw.

Snow had drifted against the tree, and the horse was buried up to his shoulder. McKay began digging, working his hands the way dogs do, while the horse looked on quizzically. Blocks of snow fell away, exposing a foreleg, a shoulder, then a shuddering flank.

McKay thought about his parents, how they had been extracted from their car and pulled dead from the canal, up through a thin layer of ice that broke over his mother's head in long translucent staves; how her gray hair had come unbraided and floated like seagrass. He remembered his father's wounded, wistful eyes—how they had still been open and when he went to close them with his own hand he couldn't; how the lariat, always kept on the front seat of his parents' car in strict coils had opened across his father's chest as if to spell out one last cry of dismay: Oooooooo.

Snow fell from the horse's back and knees. The whites of his eyes shone, and he worked his ears. McKay grabbed the rein and led the horse from the collapsed drift. He sighed deeply, then his head fell into his blue hands, and he cried.

* * *

When McKay reached the ranch no lights were on. He lit an oil lamp and wandered through the house. The snow in the living room had been mopped up—Bobby must be home. The photograph of McKay's parents had been set on the mantle over the stone fireplace and three sticks of incense were still burning.

McKay went upstairs. The old pine staircase creaked. He opened the door of the bedroom where Madeleine had slept the week before and set the lamp on a small table. For a long time he stared at the unmade bed. Then he took off all his clothes, pulled the blankets back and rubbed his aching, lonely body on the sheets where she had been.

4

THURSDAYS
AT SNUFF'S

Suddenly I saw the cold and rook-delighting heaven
That seemed as though ice burned and was the more ice,
And thereupon imagination and heart were driven
So wild that every casual thought of that and this
Vanished and left but memories, that should be out of
season
With the hot blood of youth, of love crossed long
ago . . .

—W.B. Yeats
(From "The Cold Heaven")

BRIGHT FLOODLIGHTS shone down on the mill at night, on the long dusty sheds, the front loaders, and railroad sidings. Sunrise lay pink across great mounds of tailings and left again so that by mid-morning the mineral looked white. The mill was located at a bend in a road that came from nothing and led to nothing for a hundred miles. The only other structure was a bar across the road called Snuff's Place. Between the two, human lives were caught and suspended the way floating tree branches become snagged on sandbars. Snuff's took in and gave out people whose nervous, sour smell made the green paint peel prematurely, and the mill's pink dust blew back over the gaunt building as if to conceal its ramshackle edifice and clothe it decently.

Out back an archipelago of small cabins made a line up the hill. In the twenties, they had housed the only black madam in the state and her three employees, though after a few years, because business there was brisker, they moved back to Butte, Montana where they had come from . When the Depression hit Snuff opened the cabins again, fitted the beds with worn but clean blankets and let jobless men and women coming through on freights sleep in them.

Now only one cabin was occupied. Someone called the Wildman lived there. He had fallen from a moving train just beyond the mill on a forty below zero night and when he was found, the tops of his ears had to be cut off because of frostbite. After, he stayed. At the height of the Depression he was seen acting as Snuff's chauffeur, parodying the decorous door-openings and gestures though both men wore rags.

In the one uncurtained window at the end of the bar, shaped like a porthole, a geranium plant laden with double blossoms pressed at the grimy pane. Its gnarled stalks bent over themselves, straining to soak up the autumn light. From there Snuff watched for Carol Lyman's car every Thursday. When he saw her coupe glide in under the bloodshot pulse of the bar's neon sign, he snapped on his bow tie and poured the Manhattan he had mixed for her into a stemmed cocktail glass.

Thursdays were Carol Lyman's declared "days of freedom," days on which she donned the darkest dark glasses and assumed an air of anonymity so complete she hardly knew herself. Sometimes she walked in the badlands, collecting rocks in dry washes, or when she had enough gas she'd drive to another town and drink a milkshake at a drive-in restaurant there. She thought of her ability to step out of routine as a discipline—the way some women her age do volunteer work or take up ballet.

Carol Lyman came to Wyoming in the summer of 1941. It was already the fall of 1942 and still no one knew her well. She had arrived husbandless, with a pear-shaped retarded son, and she wasn't questioned about her past. If there had been a son, certainly there had been a husband, though his whereabouts and fate were unknown.

She took part-time jobs at the shipping yard cafe and the Heart Mountain Relocation Camp and lived in a house on the very edge of the small town of Luster. The neighbors next door had a yard full of roosters who awakened her each morning. They strutted and crowed and brawled until Manuel came out and fed them. Carol looked like a bird herself. She had long arms and legs and gnarled toes and the skin on her neck showed gooseflesh in winter. Yet she had a handsome, haughty presence, a posture that was never less than regal, and carefully kept red fingernails.

She began going to Snuff's the day the Mormon women invited her to their Relief Society Meeting. They had felt sorry for her and because wartime heightens peoples' sense of community — in direct proportion to their experience of bereavement — the women issued an invitation to the solitary Carol Lyman. She attended once. To show her gratitude she baked a banana cake and made a gallon of nonalcoholic punch, but she sat back as the women made Christmas ornaments and never joined in. During a break she went outside to have a smoke. From behind a currant bush she watched the kindly women reconvene. They kept looking up, expecting her to return. Instead she stubbed out her cigarette and drove north with her dark glasses on. That was a Thursday. She decided she would be obligated to no one from that Thursday on.

Carol drove to Snuff's on a whim. She was a guarded person who realized she had nothing to guard: her life had become as narrow as a pine needle. Snuff's bar straddled two state lines and was the loneliest place she had ever seen. That's what made her stop there.

The first time, she stepped out of the car, straightened

her hair, took a deep breath, and walked in. A chandelier in the center of the room swung in the draft of the opened door. Its bottom tier was bent and only four crystal prisms remained. A long cord descended through the middle of the fixture and a bare bulb hung down in the room like a punching bag. She walked to the middle of the floor and turned slowly. It was a big drafty place with a cream-colored tin ceiling blackened by soot. A sour smell moved stiffly through the air and mixed with something antiseptic. Flannel curtains with scenes of ducks, and hunters pointing their shotguns hung limply over unwashed windows, and the ten by ten linoleum dance floor was badly stained. There were tables and chairs and spittoons randomly arranged and at the back, a card table sparsely padded with green felt. Snuff stood between the cherrywood backbar and the marred counter where cowboys had carved their brands with pocketknives.

"You want to buy the outfit?" Snuff asked jovially, "Or do you want a drink?"

Carol Lyman turned to him. He was tall and dapper and nearing fifty. He wore a trimmed mustache and his hair rose in a wild tuft at the top of his skull. His bright eyes danced, and when he smiled, his thin lips turned white.

"A Manhattan," Carol said. "Do you know how to make one?"

Snuff looked askance and went to work. He poured and shook and strained and in a moment held out the drink she had requested. She ate the cherry first, returned the stem, then drained the glass of its reddish-orange liquid.

"Very good. Thank you," she said, handed Snuff the correct change, and left the bar.

* * *

During the week, between one Thursday and the next, Carol Lyman put in time at her two jobs. Every morning she drove her son Willard to the grocery store where he swept floors and dusted canned goods. She watched as he careened down aisles with a wide broom and scattered fresh sawdust behind the polished butcher's case, while above his head cones of string spun and bounced on their spindles and were threaded down through black eyelets to the counter, then wound around white packages of meat.

It was shipping time, and the cafe was crowded. Sugar and coffee had been added to the list of rationed foods and were considered two of the worst small sacrifices, though when the coffeepot emptied early in the day, no one complained. The outer ring of world misery—the Death March in Bataan, the war in North Africa, Nazi burnings and killings, the arrest of Ghandi—gyrated around local commotions: the accident in which Pinkey was hit by a car; the arrival of more Japanese Americans in guarded trains; cockfights and violent snowstorms; and the coming home of the war dead.

The next free day—Thursday—Carol drove directly to Snuff's. She had not intended to, but that's where she ended up. When Snuff saw her black coupe glide in he made a pitcher of Manhattans. Just inside the door Carol pulled a compact from her purse, primped her brittle hair, then proceeded to the bar. When she saw the drink waiting for her, she gave Snuff a hesitant, surprised smile.

"How very sweet," she said and slid onto the barstool one hip at a time.

"Hello. I'm Snuff," the tall man said.

"Carol Lyman," she said, then felt the stiffness leave her body. "It's legal to gamble in Montana, isn't it?"

"More or less."

"I'd like a card game. Is that possible?"

Snuff looked at the woman quizzically. Then he snapped on his red bow tie, for luck he said, and led her to the table at the back of the room. A pool of light lay on the green felt like a full moon. Snuff opened a new deck. His bony fingers were so long they seemed to wrap twice around the cards. He shuffled, she cut, he dealt, she asked for a card, and when she turned her hand face up he saw that she had won.

She raised the stakes for the next game and the next and won again. By mid-afternoon the pile of chips in front of her had grown tall. She looked at Snuff and started laughing self-consciously.

"I can't take all this," she said, pushing the chips back toward him, and left the bar.

*   *   *

During the week snow blanketed the northern part of the state and there was a bad ground blizzard. The canary and saffron aspen leaves froze prematurely, blackened on the limb and were blown unceremoniously to the ground. One rancher brought his steers off the mountain through the middle of town. They trampled rose bushes and vegetable gardens, ran onto one old woman's front porch, right into her living room. Then the weather turned warm.

Thursday morning Carol Lyman drove to the badlands behind her house. Wild horses ranged there in the fall and she hoped to catch a glimpse of them. She followed a road so faint it sometimes disappeared and the tops of the sagebrush scratched the underside of her car. Finally she stopped, got out, and knelt down. The white scarf she wore, a present from a man she loved twenty years before, whipped her face. In front of her were the cold hoofprints of horses. They overlapped and moved out from under her body as if running from her. The wind howled. When she looked up she saw the sky had turned violet-black — the color of a bruise. Hail fell. She pulled the scarf over her head and tied it tightly. Hail battered the back of her head and when the wind shifted suddenly it beat on her face. She stood, put on her dark glasses and drove away. Behind her the horsetracks, carved into soft soil, filled with white stones.

She arrived at Snuff's in the early afternoon. As she unwound the white scarf from her neck and head she thought it was like taking off a bandage. Her cocktail teetered on the scarred counter. The liquid swung from side to side and where it ran down the glass it left an orange residue that looked like gasoline. Snuff watched Carol drink. The dimples that showed when he smiled gave him a youthful, mischievous look. They took their usual places at the blackjack table and Carol won every game.

When the bar door swung open the chandelier swung slightly. A short man on crutches hobbled to the middle of the floor. His gray Stetson was cocked sideways on his head.

"What can I do for you, Pinkey?" Snuff asked.

"Ooooooooweee. Look at all that money," he exclaimed.

"It's hers," Snuff said flatly.

Pinkey doffed his hat to Carol. One of the crutches fell from under his arm as he did so.

"I need a saw," Pinkey said.

"What in hell kind of drink is that?"

Pinkey squinted hard at the tall man. "Well you're dumber than I thought you was. What's wrong, don't you savvy English?"

Snuff grinned.

"You've got to get me outta this sonofabitch, that's what I mean," Pinkey said and kicked his broken leg into the air.

When Snuff refilled Carol's glass Pinkey peered over the rim.

"What's that hummin' bird food you're drinkin'?" he asked.

"Here, try it," she said.

"Hell no, that'd clog up my pipes."

Carol inspected the mutilated cast. It was blotched with mud and the bottom edge was badly frayed.

"How long have you had that on?" she asked.

"Too long . . . a couple of weeks, I guess."

Snuff disappeared and came back carrying a meat saw.

"What are you going to do with *that*?" Carol asked.

"Pinkey, lay back on that big table over there, will you?" Snuff said. "Carol, grab his heel and kinda steady the thing."

Pinkey lay back on the long oak table, a relic from the neighboring town's one lawyer who died and whose office sat idle for twelve years. Pinkey watched as the saw sank into white plaster. Soon the cast was halved, and Snuff pried it apart. They peered down at the leg.

"God it looks wormy, don't it?" Pinkey said. "Can't you put that thing back on?"

Snuff held a piece of the cast up and laughed.

"Then get me a shot of whiskey," Pinkey said.

Snuff brought the drink and Pinkey gulped it down. He slid off the table slowly until both feet, the one with the boot on and the pale one covered by a sock, touched the floor. He put weight on the broken leg, then lifted it gingerly. He tried again. Then he looked at Snuff, and at his foot.

"I'm healed. I'm healed," he cried and waved his crutches in the air like wings. He stood up. The leg held.

"Just send me a bill, Snuff," he said and hooked the crutches on the chandelier's bent frame. They watched as he hobbled out the door.

Carol Lyman turned on her heel and gasped. The Wildman stood directly behind her. Clean-shaven, his black hair was long and matted. He had olive skin and a dappling of black moles—beauty spots—on his jaw, a dent that flattened the bridge of his nose, and penetrating eyes.

"What are you afraid of?" he asked.

In confusion, Carol looked imploringly at Snuff.

"Carol, that's the Wildman. He lives out back," Snuff said quietly.

"My dog is sick. Maybe you can help him," the Wild-man said.

Carol nodded, and she and Snuff followed the man to the cabin. Inside it was cramped but tidy. A narrow bed had been shoved up against one wall, a steamer trunk against another, and, leaning sideways, there was a tall bookcase crammed with a miscellany of titles: *The Virginian*, *War and Peace*, and a set of *World Book Encyclopedias* and a stack of 1942 *Saturday Evening Posts*.

Carol looked at the dog. A kelpie, used for working livestock, he was smaller than a wolf but with a wolfish nose and ears.

"I found him abandoned in an irrigation ditch. He was just a little rat, a few days old. I guess they tried to drown him, but someone forgot to turn the water on," the Wildman explained.

"Let's take him to the bar where he'll be warm," Snuff said.

The Wildman bundled the dog in a torn blanket and carried him to the green building. Carol had not noticed before but the afternoon was nearly gone. In the north-west dark clouds humped up and moved toward this desolate bend in the road. Despite heavy snows the week before, the air felt tropical and Carol thought she could smell the sea.

They made a soft bed for the dog under the oak table where he had always liked to sleep. He gave them a grateful, sad look. Snuff went to the porthole window and looked outside. In the distance lightning domed the dark sky with its ghostly hood of light. There was a terrible explosion of thunder overhead. Then the lights in the bar went out.

"Snuff. What's happening?"

Snuff pressed his face against the grimy porthole. Outside it was dark too: the neon light off, the mill dark, no moon. The door swung open. A small figure stood in the entry and did not move.

"Come on in," Snuff said.

Still the visitor remained motionless.

"Who's there?" Snuff asked again.

When there was no answer Snuff came out from behind the bar and fell once against the bottles.

"Snuff, goddamn it, can't you light a match or something?" Carol yelled. She heard a match being struck behind her, then another. The Wildman held up a silver candelabra.

"Where did you get a thing like that?" Carol whispered as they approached the silent figure at the door. A wizened Japanese man appeared before them. When the light shone on his face, he hid his head in his hands. Then he regained his composure.

"They leave me. Cannot find way back. So confused . . ." he began.

"Who left you?" Snuff asked. "Are you Japanese or American?"

The old man looked at Snuff timidly but gave no answer. Snuff took the candelabra from the Wildman and went to the phone. The line was dead. He put the receiver back slowly.

"Christ," he mumbled, then rejoined the others.

A plane flew over. It made a high uneven whine that deepened into a drone as it veered away. Snuff and Carol looked up at the ceiling. Then they heard a car and two gunshots.

"What's going on around here?" Snuff said. "Maybe we better find some cover for awhile."

"Oh Snuff . . ." Carol protested, but when Snuff led the old man away from the door, Carol and the Wildman followed. Snuff helped the old man down and they all joined the sick dog under the great oak table.

"Here, give me that light," Carol said and held the candelabra up to the old man. Under coal black eyebrows he had an elfish face and a delicate upswinging nose. Gray hair was swept back from a long, grooved forehead.

"I know you," she said. "From the Camp."

"Hai. Heart Mountain. Hai," he replied cheerfully and broke into a timid smile.

"You better blow those out now," Snuff said quietly.

The Wildman held the dog close to him, and in the dark they could hear the animal's labored breathing. Another plane droned overhead. This one was farther away.

"War and peace," the Wildman whispered and chuckled at his private joke.

In the confusion Carol's hand touched Snuff's under the folds of a coat he had thrown down for them and she did not move it away. They braced themselves, though for what they weren't sure—for a bomb to be dropped, for a Japanese army to burst in, for sudden death. Snuff positioned himself so he could see out the porthole at the end of the bar. Beyond the bent geranium the sky was a blank. Even the north star, the axis around which the other stars revolved, had been obscured.

Carol leaned back against the table's thick pedestal. It was like a tree, she thought, the trunk curved and smooth and branching into a sheltering canopy. For a moment the window went white with lightning. A clap of thunder jangled the chandelier's crystal prisms. Carol imagined she was on a boat. Wind whistled and the air slipping under the door into the stale room smelled of a failing sun and seaweed.

They waited. Each tried to comfort the dog, passing him from lap to lap, stroking his hair. When the dog was passed to the old man, Carol whispered, "He's just old. There's nothing to be afraid of." Then she looked at the man again. "I'm Carol Lyman," she said.

"Nakamura. Hello," the old man replied.

"Where did you relocate from?" she asked.

"Los Angeles. I was a flower grower. Then had to come here. Plant garden. No good, no grow," he said forlornly.

The Wildman looked at him. "Nothing grows here except cactus, rattlesnakes and jackrabbits," he said dryly.

Mr. Nakamura gave the dog back and looked the Wildman in the eye. "Maybe he die tonight," he said.

"Yes," the Wildman said and rocked the dog tenderly in his arms.

*   *   *

The night was divided by long silences and short interludes of whispered talk. Snuff spoke first. He told of an upbringing in the mining town Butte.

"I worked for Marcus Daley. He owned just about everything in Anaconda and Butte. Besides the mines he had a big hotel. It was quite a place. Everything in it was made of copper—even the toilet seats. All kinds of people came through: boxers, opera singers, movie stars, gangsters. They said Butte was an island of easy money entirely surrounded by whiskey. I was an orphan. My dad died in the mines. Oh, death was common. One man died every day in those mines; the cemetery held forty thousand. Money was easy; death was easy. I guess it was living that got to be hard.

"I grew up on Venus Alley. Do you know what that was? A whole street of whorehouses. When Mr. Daley put me to work I didn't have a dime. He taught me something about making money. I even had a little string of race horses all my own. Then I lost them in a poker game. And in exchange I got this place."

Snuff paused and looked at his surroundings, then laughed.

"I think of myself as a priest in a hardship post. I might have had a gentleman's life, but things get lost along the way," he said wearily.

Snuff's story was followed by silence. The rumbling of the Wildman's stomach broke the spell. Carol smothered a laugh, then crawled on hands and knees behind the bar. She returned with a handful of elk jerky and four pickled eggs. They were shared by all. The Wildman broke his egg in half and gave the yolk to his dog.

"What about you?" Carol asked, looking at the Wildman.

He smiled and his dark eyes bounced like wild berries stripped from a green vine.

"I fell out of a boxcar across the road. Snuff took me in."

Carol looked at him intently. "Is that *all*?"

The Wildman's eyes widened. Then he shrugged and continued.

"My ears were frostbitten. After I healed up and

spring came I commenced to work as an irrigator. It's a job, like child's play. I like water. You can't hang onto it. You have to keep letting go."

A silence followed. All eyes were on the Wildman. His matted hair sprouted straight up from his head as if he were electrified.

"Before that I was enrolled at a place called Harvard. One day I came home from class and my house had been robbed. Then I looked out at the streets and I knew why. It was the thirties, I had lots of things and other people had nothing. I wanted to know what it was like to be poor, so I rode the rails. When I returned, my parents had lost everything. I wanted to spare them the embarrassment of having an extra mouth to feed so I took off again and landed here."

Carol's head dropped. For a moment tears stood in her eyes and dropped at an angle away from her face like a pair of dice. The small dog groaned, stretched his back legs and collapsed again in the Wildman's lap. Snuff looked through the window. Two stars shone, then one was overtaken by clouds.

"I wonder what's happening out there," Snuff said.

The Wildman looked at him. "Nothing. The lights went out, that's all. Who would bomb this desiccated piece of real estate anyway? Did you ever think of that?"

No one answered.

"What about you, Mr. Nakamura?" Carol said.

The old man looked at her timidly. "Oh no, is no very good story."

"All stories are good," she said.

He looked from one to the other, then sat up straight and began.

"I come on ship. I'm opposite him," he said and pointed to the Wildman. "I start out with nothing. Come her to make money. Ship take long time. Very rough. People sick all over. Only one other man on board. All others—women. Picture brides. You know them? Mail order. They have photograph of man they marry. That's all. Never meet before. Just picture. Well, one woman, she so scared she jump overboard. Then her friend and I fall in love. She very beautiful. We write poems to each other every day. Like in Heian times. The day we are coming to port, we don't know what we will do. She stand in bow of ship all day looking at picture of her man. As soon as we see land, she tear it and throw it to the birds. When we get off boat, there he is. Right in front. Oh, so ashamed. She grab my arm like married woman and we walk by. It is very bad thing we do, but in those days, love matches not very common. Not common at all.

"After, I work for farmer. Then lease own land. Very beautiful. Right on coast, hill overlook ocean. Like Japan. We grow daisies. Many, many acres of them. So thick, I think they look like snow."

The Wildman rearranged the ailing dog and covered

him with a torn blanket. Carol thought of all the places these people had lived; how they looked as if a river had run through them and swept all the small comforts away. Because it was dark in the bar, her eyes were closed sometimes, sometimes open. Maybe she would die tonight, she thought, flanked by three strange men. Yet her body felt light. She had not touched any part of a man for many years and now Snuff's arm pressed firmly against her back. A fly trapped under the dog's blanket buzzed, then stopped. The dog's eyes opened, an ear twitched, then sleep overtook him again.

"Carol?" Snuff said.

"I can't."

"Why not?"

"Because I've never told anyone."

Nakamurasan looked at her. "Nothing to lose, huh?"

Carol smiled. The Wildman relit the candelabra, and their faces glowed. Carol cleared her throat.

"I spent a summer near here twenty years ago. I was young and had come to stay at a ranch. In August there was a party at a ranch on the other side of the mountain. We started out on horseback and rode all day. We arrived just as the fiddle players were tuning up. It was a lovely party. Paper lanterns had been strung across the veranda and through the trees. There were tables and tables of food. Everyone came. Even the sheepherders. I remember how they stood at the door and wouldn't come in at first. They had their dogs with them.

"During the evening I wandered down a long hall into another part of the house. I heard someone coughing, so I peeked in. A young man was lying in bed. He was the handsomest man I had ever seen. He had thick, wavy hair the color of chocolate and a straight nose and big glowing eyes. Every feature was perfect. He looked like a young god lying there. He told me he had pneumonia. His cheeks were very flushed, and he kept clutching my hand and asking me to stay there and talk to him. So I did. We talked about everything—there seemed to be no inhibitions. I had never talked that way to a man before. Only once did someone come in and check on him. We were alone for the rest of the night."

Carol paused, then continued.

"He was the father of Willard. I say 'was' because he died a week later. I saw it in the paper the day I was leaving to go home."

Carol looked at the others. All at once the arbitrariness of their lives seemed absurd. This bend in the road and the little towns on either side, linked by great acreages of desolation, had neither accepted nor refused them. There was room here, that was all—a geographical accident. What they had done, how far they had drifted was of no concern. The convulsions of weather and seasons would always be greater than they were. That was a comfort too, Carol thought. The bigness and strangeness of the landscape had acted on he like a drug and try as she did to reason why any of them had ended up here, she could push no clear idea into her mind.

She felt tired and cold suddenly and lay her head against Snuff's knee. A warm wind rattled the doors and windows of the bar. After awhile she slipped into a light sleep. She dreamed she was on a boat, though the seaswells she thought cradled her were Snuff's arms and the back legs of the dying dog and the Wildman's knees and Nakamura's folded hands. The boat passed over a school of fish. Then she could see herself from up in the air as though she were flying. It was not water that held the boat, but light. A clap of thunder woke her.

"What time is it?" she asked startled.

Snuff looked toward the grimy window and shrugged. Rain undulated across the darkened mill, slapped at the road and against the windowpanes, then ceased. A car drove by. There were three gunshots this time. The Wildman stood up excitedly and ran out the door, shaking the candelabra like a staff. A smell of wet sage tumbled into the room as if it had been accumulating there for years. He ran to the middle of the road and yelled: "Here I am . . . here I am. Can you see me? Shoot me. Go ahead. You can have me. Come on," he said, taunting an empty sky. As he spoke, wind extinguished the candles one by one.

Carol and Snuff went after him. A wide band of red stretched across the eastern horizon and the black began to drain from the sky. Each took an arm and led the Wildman back to the bar. Nakamura was holding the dog and singing something in Japanese. The dog's body had stiffened; he was dead.

The Wildman knelt in front of the old man and put his head to the dog's chest. After, he sat up limply. Carol put her arm around him, and when he turned his head into her shoulder they could hear his muffled sobs. Carol's eyes passed over the Wildman's clotted hair and met Snuff's. They had never really looked at one another. She felt as if her body were being pressed through a screen, the soft parts flowing forward. The screen was a last restraint beyond which there were only openings.

When Snuff looked through the porthole, he saw daylight. Simultaneously, they got to their feet and went outside. The red belt of first light had widened: it looked like a pink shield held up to do battle with night. The sky was neither blue nor black, but pale as if the gases had been burned from it. The Wildman walked away from the others. They watched as he clambered up the pink dune of mineral tailings: over the lip of one, down the backside, up another. Nakamura pointed to the mounds.

"They are the color of fallen cherry blossoms," he said. Carol looked at the wizened old man. She thought she had never seen a morning like that, a more exquisite bend in the road. She wrapped her long arms around herself and felt ribs under her sweater. Trembling from the cold that comes just before sunrise, she rocked back and forth on her feet. Snuff looked at her.

"You look like a bride," he said.

The pink came out of the sky all at once. Now the cherry blossoms looked like drifted snow. The air took on a transparency like the hottest part of a flame. She thought she could see the stories she had heard that night skittering above the horizon, the troublesome human parts — the pain and blame — burning into the blandness of day.

A car barreled down the highway toward them. It was Pinkey and two other cowboys. They waved wildly as they passed, then the one in the back seat drew a pistol and shot three times into the air.

Perched on a pink mound, all the candles escaped from the candelabra. The Wildman started laughing. He lay on his side and rolled from the crest to the bottom of the mound and stood up at Carol's feet, his face and hair powdered thickly with dust. He did not brush himself off but walked towards the bar, his shoulders drooping slightly. As Carol, Snuff and Nakamura followed, the neon sign over the door buzzed suddenly, lit up and began its habitual blinking once again.

PART II:

After the War

5

MADELEINE'S DAY

I DON'T KNOW what took me over that September day—the day Henry came home from being a prisoner of war in Japan—but I sped off on my horse and hid behind a hill. It was a cruel thing to do and perhaps my cruelty did not end there since it has a way of striking again and again. He had not come straight home from the Camp, but from the decks of the ship, *Missouri*, where he and other officers witnessed the signing of the surrender, then stateside from a Seattle hospital. What I'm getting at is that I was expecting him to be in better shape than he was, but that's getting ahead of the story.

As soon as I saw him standing at the gate and heard his two-fingered whistle, I hurried back to him, yet when we finally embraced, his presence was like a wind trying to blow me away. Was it his fear or mine? I don't know, but no matter what we did we could not seem to get close. For months I had been rehearsing our first night together, our first meal. That's what four years of war reduces you to—menus and place settings—but I

95

finally decided on T-bone steaks, fried potatoes with a little onion, the wild asparagus I picked last spring and a lemon meringue pie.

After he put his things down, he followed me into the kitchen. I had already sweated two half moons into my shirt because there was nothing and everything to talk about. It either sounded too trivial or too serious for the first night at home. I took up the slack by cooking.

When it came time to eat he was hungry but couldn't make himself cut into the steak.

"I haven't had anything like this for a long time," he said. "I want it, but my stomach's afraid."

I guess I hadn't anticipated this problem, in fact I hadn't anticipated anything at all. His coming home was all that had mattered, and it was only natural to welcome him with a big spread because less would have seemed paltry.

He ate a few forkfuls, smiled at me, slowly pushed away, and threw up halfway to the back door.

That was the first and last time for many months that we tried to have a real dinner. What was wrong with me, why hadn't I known it would be like this?

I cooked up some rice and chicken broth and fed him in bed like a baby. After, he slept and I sat at the kitchen table and ate my enormous, stupid meal alone.

For the next few months I couldn't bring myself to share the same bed. That first night I stayed up late and thumbed through our old wedding pictures, though I knew it was into the future I should have been looking. My mother had warned me about "re-entry problems" which she said I must face with the same bravery I'd faced running the ranch alone, but I found this more difficult by far.

I slept on the couch then went out early the next morning to move cows. It was time to start bringing them closer to the ranch for winter. On my return I found Henry waiting for me, showered and dressed, thin and pale.

"I'm sorry about last night," he said. "It was a magnificent dinner. It's what I would have asked for."

He wanted to ride so I caught a horse, a gentle one I had bought during the war, and we rode out to the pasture so he could see the cattle. It occurred to me that many of these mother cows had been born while he was away. As he asked me about them, who their mother had been and where I'd bought bulls, it was like having a visitor at the ranch. Nothing of the old feeling was there, of the shared effort it takes to bring a herd along through winter and calving and summer storms. Only one thought ran through my head: these were the cattle McKay and I had raised.

Henry was too weak to ride fourteen-hour days in bad weather, and I had no idea how long that would go on. So he occupied his days making my small vegetable garden into a bigger one, hauling wheelbarrows of manure one by one and raking it in. One day he worked right through a September storm, heavy snow breaking branches all around and no matter how much time he put in, it would be eight months before he could plant seeds. He looked like a living skeleton.

It was then that I understood why war zones are called "theatres" because they frame a kind of play acting or, worse, deceit, that can stain a human life forever: the deceit of hate on hearsay—hating an enemy one doesn't know—and the deceit of a disrupted marriage inside of which a dark cavity grows. Yet, as the weeks went by I think I gained patience because I knew that in the natural geography of a marriage, love goes all over the place and the vows suspend disbelief until two people hook up again or go their separate ways.

One day I rode in early. The sky had been clouding over and a cold wind was pushing down from the Arctic. Henry always said he could hear the polar bears yawning when a north wind blew. But that day it was only him I heard.

"Don't come in here," he yelled as I opened the gate.

He was weeping, not in short bursts but in a low drone. I went to him anyway. He had on only a T-shirt, and it had begun to snow. I held him for a long time. He wedged the hoe between us as if to fend me off, to drive comfort away.

"So many of them died no matter what I did," he said. But that was all.

It was around Thanksgiving when I found the food he had been hoarding under the bed: peanut butter, crackers, canned goods, coffee. Since that day in the garden I learned he and the other men had bribed a guard for vegetable seeds and grown a huge garden at the Camp and had been responsible for keeping everyone, guards and prisoners both, from starving. I didn't say anything about the food. What difference did it make? The slightest misunderstanding might upset his progress. He'd just begun to fill out his clothes.

At least that's what I thought was right, when truly, I had no idea. Nine weeks had gone by since he had come home. That's a long time to live with a stranger. Finally, I called Bobby Korematsu because he knew how to take care of people. McKay answered the phone. His voice surprised me and my face flushed. We hadn't talked for a long time.

"At least you could come over and see me once in a while," he said.

"I know. I'm sorry. It's just that Henry's not doing too well."

"You better come then," he said, and I did, that very day.

I wanted to take Henry because he had seen McKay only once and they had been — despite everything — such good friends, but Henry said, "No, you go." Maybe that's when the cruelty began, because I went ahead without him. He watched me leave, his hands and chin resting on the hoe handle. When I ran over to blow him a kiss, the skin around his eyes tightened. Was he the prisoner and I the guard? How easily he acquiesced, but what could I expect? He had not known anything else for four years.

It felt good to drive fast. I knew the dirt track between our ranch and McKay's without having to think. I opened the windows, unsnapped my jacket and breathed in the chilled air. Home, I'm going home, I found myself thinking . . .

Bobby was nowhere to be found, nor was McKay. Champ's blue roan was in the corral. He eyed me, arched his neck and snorted. Then McKay appeared and before I knew what was happening we were laughing and hugging and I pushed my knee between his legs.

"Ain't you a sight for sore eyes," he said.

"Ain't?"

"Don't start that . . ." he said winking.

"Why are your eyes sore?" I asked. "Who have you been looking at?"

"Heifers," he said. "The kind with four legs."

Then we embraced, only this time I wasn't laughing and a hard knot came all the way up through my body from my stomach into my throat like an old cow's cud made of tears. I bit my lip.

"Come on inside," McKay said, gently leading me into the house as he had done that night so many years ago, the night I found out Henry had been taken prisoner of war.

McKay poured coffee and added a shot of brandy. I watched him watch me drink. He saw into me. I said I missed him which is what we always say to each other, only usually, it's him saying it to me.

Are we so weak-hearted that we can only dive backward to what we know, to what we were? Or was history twisting me like a flower following the sun of McKay? Bobby never did come back that afternoon, and I'm not sure if I can say what happened. In some ways nothing did and that was the beauty of it. Since the end of the war, the whole world had become addicted to resuming normality. Few of us had been able to keep up the pace. "Normal times" were always a couple of lengths away and we secretly knew our valiant efforts had been failures.

I'd thought certain things had come to an end in my life, specifically, the cat-and-mouse game I'd always played with McKay, and in a way it had. But something else had taken its place, something even now I'm not sure of. Before, I was always reacting to him: pulling away or throwing myself into his life. Now, we were both too tired for such things.

That afternoon we sat quietly together at the kitchen table, nothing else. Yet, I felt I belonged there. McKay was his usual brooding, beautiful self. The wind howled and the stovepipe rattled in the ceiling. After a long time, he started pacing, circling me noiselessly as if marking out on the floor the distance that had kept us apart, trying to trample it away.

I left at four in the afternoon. I'd already been gone longer than I should have, and it was beginning to snow.

I found Henry in the bathroom. In front of him were boxes of food, opened, half-eaten. He gave me a fearful look as if I might scold him. I don't know how long I stood there staring at him and he at me, like two deer frozen in front of headlights. I remembered his story about being parachuted onto an island with no food. How in his hours of waiting for the maneuvre to begin, he drew pictures of roasts and pies in the sand with a stick because it was Christmas Day.

He stuck his hand into a jar and took out a handful of pickled beans. When he offered them to me, I could no longer contain myself and burst out laughing.

"I'm hungry," he said in a small voice. Had my laughter hurt him?

I went into the kitchen and brought back a pie, a round of Swiss cheese, a loaf of homemade bread, and carved bite-sized pieces of each, lowering myself down on the bathroom floor so that our legs were entwined and facing each other this way, we ate. The dogs scratched on the door. They wanted to join in so we let them.

"This tastes so good," Henry said, our eyes locked, mouths full of food, we trembled with laughter, trying not to choke.

Finally, he was still. His green eyes softened. When I opened my arms, he leaned toward me, almost falling as if I was sky and he was jumping from a plane.

6

PINKEY

I DIED LAST WEEK. Does that surprise you? Went over the ridge just like that, no long illness, no blizzard to get lost in, no sympathy cards, no horse wreck. Hell, I didn't even know it was coming on, I didn't know I was anything like sick. It was so warm that night I didn't have to build a fire, and the cows and calves were out on green grass for the first time since winter. I was playing solitaire. Once I stopped and stood in the doorway of the cabin and looked out across the hills that had gone from brown to green in three days, and I remember the air was so soft it was like a baby's skin laid against mine, but my baby, my kid Vincent, he'd already gone off and froze himself to death on those pink mine tailings there at Snuff's on the eve of his departure into the great U.S. Army where he probably would have died anyway since they always sent the Indian kids to the front lines. But I didn't have no send-off party like he did. In fact no one was around. I'd had the shakes real bad like always after a few good drunks. They'd started up during calving, and the cold hurt me bad, and my back was sore all the way through to the front like I was one bruise, and nothing tasted good anymore. But hell, I was just glad I'd made it to green grass. That's all a man can hope for.

After McKay and Champ left me off with the cattle, I watched a gray sheet of rain sweep through—it came all the way across the valley from Montana and danced out into the Dakotas somewhere and when it cleared off, the ground steamed. God, I wanted to saddle old Eleanor and ride out through the cattle to make sure they'd mothered up okay, but I couldn't hardly make my legs move, didn't know what was wrong, and that's when I took the deck of cards down and played half a dozen games just to take my mind off things. By things, I mean the way Vincent was dancing around in the corners of the room every which way, smooth as a cougar, and shaking his long black hair. Then my worthless old legs moved too even though I was sitting stock still. It was like I had two sets of bones and the one was dancing away from the other. Just as quick it'd stop. By then I'd played about thirty rounds of solitaire and hadn't won a damned game which was about par for the course, then there was a noise and the room felt like all the air had been sucked out of it and I wondered if it was Vincent up to something again, then it got dark and I couldn't breathe.

Maybe things would have turned out different if Bobby had been there. I believe he knew things that could have brought that extra skeleton back inside me, but that's not how the cards lay that night, not for me anyway. I keep going over it in my mind: I was laying out my cards — a six of hearts, a seven of spades, a red queen, a deuce, an ace, a nine, a jack, then a joker showed up when I took the ace off to lay it above the other cards. How it got in there I don't know, but I picked it up between my finger and thumb and flicked it onto the floor. One other thing. The dog had been nervous all day. Now, I've never made a dog uneasy in my life, that's the one thing I've been good for, getting into a dog's mind, knowing when and why he'll work for me. And there he was trying like hell to tell me I was about to kick off and I didn't even savvy what he was saying. That's how smart a dog is and how dumb a man can be.

After the room went dark it was like drinking dry clouds, the mist was going through my chest and there were leaves in my eyes, plastered inside like they were stuck to something wet. I didn't have any feet or legs but I was moving, first up at an angle then down fast at a slant toward sand, but when I hit there was no impact, no sound. I could hear my dog talk. He was trying like hell to come with me, he was whimpering, then I heard lots of other sounds all around, maybe I was making them too.

I remember McKay coming in sometime later and the

dog not letting him close which made me laugh, so the kid lay down on the floor and inched his way over to me like a submissive female dog, and when he put his head down to listen for a heartbeat I wanted to tell him I didn't have a chest anymore. It made me think of the time he and I found the little white calf born half under a fence in a blizzard, froze solid to the ground with a coyote eating on its back legs and McKay putting his head down to check if the animal was still alive, which he was, and how I took my coat off and stuffed his frozen feet into the sleeves and together we carried him to the warming room in the barn, half a mile or so, with the mother following. Stayed up all night rubbing that calf's legs and goddam, if he didn't grow up to be a thousand pound steer.

Now people are asking why I died, but that's something even I don't know. There's no such thing as why anymore or where or when. All I know is that my funeral turned out to be a hell of a party and my only regret is that I wasn't there. Sometimes I dive down into a room like a fish and blow open the windows or knock things down or make the lights go off. It's strange the way I can move, and behind me I can hear children standing one in back of the other like a row of stacked chairs, chanting like they were at a football game only they sound sad. Nobody gets it when I go through a room which I don't do too often, except for the dogs—they see me, and sometimes the horses run around, then McKay jumps up to see if it's a bear come down, but hell, it's only me.

"Did he suffer at the end?" I heard someone ask. Hell, I didn't suffer a lick as long as I had my Cobb's Creek with me, best friend a man ever had after a dog is whiskey. It was always like pouring honey over broken glass, and there was a lot of broken glass in my life . . . Like the time I tried to quit and smashed all my bottles on the rocks and got so thirsty I started licking the grass where it had spilled. Bobby told me that in Japan people were once so hungry they ate grass and leaves with their rice, but I've never been hungry like that, only thirsty, so thirsty I knew I was dying only it was worse than what dying is really like because all that glass had shattered inside me and little fires were breaking out in my throat and something hot seared both eyes.

Now I move around like I was on skates. I glide over my thirst, the blades slitting my neck a hundred times, but the only agony is the way I can see and hear my dogs talking, the way they know about a storm before there are even clouds in the sky, and could have told me which cow was going to calve next, pointed her right out to me, and other things, like when I was going to die. And I like listening to them talk among themselves. They have their own affairs to settle, their own opinions about things, and their dreams are like long ribbons of green water which they run on. Sometimes I dive down and try to catch one or two of them. If I could just run my hand along their backs, under their chests, and smell their tangy breath and feel their smooth tongues on my face . . . but they keep slipping away.

7

KAI'S MOTHER

AKEMASHITE OMEDETO GOZAIMASU. Happy New Year. It makes me think of the New Year of 1945 when the camp director told us we were free to leave. War not even over. So why did they say we could go home if we couldn't go before? Americans think funny about things like they were born in a time when the seasons were all mixed up. No thought follows directly after the other. Just like my boy, Kai. He's getting that way too. That's why when he said, "Let's go back to California now," I said no. They'll shoot us down like inu, like dogs.

Maaa . . . but it was so hard. Watched many friends leave. Made me think of home, smell of eucalyptus trees, gold light on bay. But where we go anyway? We lost our house. Treasury froze our money, Kai said, can't make payments. Anyway, bad stories came back to Camp about California. Won't let Japanese live anywhere, only slave work in fields, sleep in sheds on wet ground like we did when we first arrived here.

Then the war did end and Japan surrendered. I

remember listening to the radio when the Emperor's voice came on. I did not understand how that could be possible, that the Emperor could talk to us that way. What shame I felt. Kai came running. Wanted to celebrate. That's what I mean about him. What he says doesn't make sense. No respect. Couldn't even see I didn't want to talk.

Finally they made us leave. Camps all close down forever. We were there such long time, didn't seem possible. My husband had to be carried like a baby to the train. His mind had gone and there was nothing to be done for him. We left on the train just the way we had come except Kai wasn't with us now, he'd been called into the Army, and they sent him to Minnesota, to language school. Imagine, Kai learning Japanese! Even Father thought that was funny.

Four years is a long time to be in one place and it's hard to make a change, but the farther we got from Heart Mountain, the more joyful I became. "We are going back to America," I kept saying, but my husband who was much older than me was "shorito"—one of those who didn't believe Japan had been defeated. All he could think about was the old Japan. But old Japan not always so good. I came from farm in north. Many times didn't have enough to eat. My mother had one baby after another. She was so tired. Wrapped them in straw coats and put them on floor in front of fire. Some died. Not strong enough for that kind of cold. I helped bury them. One of my sisters was born blind. She was taken away when she was twelve to become "itako"—one who calls back the dead. When she came home five years later, she looked like old woman. Scared me. Told her to go away because dead spirits can climb on your back and you can never get rid of them. I worked in rice fields with my mother and father and helped cook meals.

I was happy to leave there. I was sent for by a relative in Aomori. It was an arranged marriage, everyone's was. He was farmer too, but he heard about going to America, make more money, so he went, then I go too. The boat was terrible. So rough and raining all the time. One picture bride got in trouble with a sailor. Tore up picture of husband and hid below. Stayed on ship all that time it was docked, and sailed back to Japan. Her husband searched, but never found her.

When people say, "Watch out. The Americans will hate you when you get out of Camps," I didn't worry. I saw worse things in Japan, like the mountain behind our village where outcasts lived: cripples and lepers. That's how it was there. If something was wrong with you, you were sent to that place. Some nights my father went gambling up there. Saw him go with lantern in hand and barrel of saké strapped to his back. Got those poor people drunk, then cheated at hanafuda. Now I know it was wrong, but then I was too hungry to care.

Sometime before we arrived in Oakland — we were still crossing the mountains — I woke up and felt my husband shaking me. "Where are we? Are we in Aomori-ken?" I tried to explain, but he couldn't listen. As we came down out of the Sierra he kept naming mountains in Japan: Hakkodayama, Iwakiyama, Yudono. Then he said, "We won, didn't we?" and I said, "Yes, America won the war." He shook his head, no. Finally dozed off. I knew then that our future was in my hands. What would we do when we arrived? Where would we go? I thought about Kai. He is American boy, what would he say to do?

I knew my husband was no good for work. I would call our Danish neighbor first about the things he was keeping for us, then I'd call the Buddhist church if it still existed. We could go there for the night. Many women had gone into domestic service in San Francisco. I knew I could do that, or I could go down to my husband's relatives in Guadalupe and work in the strawberry fields.

Our old life was gone. No more house in Richmond, but I didn't care. So much had changed, better to make what they call, clean sweep. I had learned things at Heart Mountain — that my husband would not be able to help me anymore, that my sons could hate each other even if they had the same blood, and all that talk about being American or being Japanese didn't matter now. I listened to the train. It was like a clock, clicking away the miles, clicking away the years.

Just before we pulled into the station I held my husband's wrist. For a moment I couldn't feel a pulse. Was he dead? Funny, but I wasn't scared. Then a long ropey pulse came, and his eyelids fluttered. "We're home now," I said. When the train doors opened, all I could smell was eucalyptus. To the west a bank of fog rolled over the ocean like an arm dividing Japan from me, poured in under bridges, eating the pink edge of the continent, then exploded against the train, taking with it my fear.

8

HENRY

How many days? How much food in the house? How can I sweat when I'm cold? Have to take food inventory. At night I want to wake her up. She sleeps on the couch. Thinks what I have is catching. She sleeps through everything. Stopped chewing my nails. Have better things to eat now, when I can eat. The body is willing, unwilling, willing. Just a taste is enough, half a teaspoon of anything—chocolate, rice, sugar, peanut butter. Madeleine on horseback, escaping me. My back hurts from puking. Will someone please turn on the lights? Okay, I'll go outside. How far is it? Where does it stop? I had a guardian angel, then one day he sneezed and poof, I vanished. All but a few bones. Got to get out of bed but can't. M. caught me hiding. Shit, there's no privacy here. I'm tired of being the freak show. In prison no one looked. We were all the same. I wish I could blow these mountains down so I could see. The dogs would come with me. They don't stare, they just go on being dogs. We could go forever, sleeping in the sun, sleeping in the snow, year around, who would care?

9

CHAMP'S ROAN COLT

I TOLD MY ROAN COLT one afternoon how I was gut shot, wounded in the leg, went goofy for a while, then sent back into action, but I didn't get any sympathy. Works on the girls, what's wrong with this damned horse? McKay can walk right out into the pasture and catch him, but me—you'd think the Loch Ness monster had just arrived. Maybe it's the cane. The goddamned wooden third leg. Can't walk. Can't stand right, can't get on a horse right, gimp, gimp, gimp. Is that what scares him? Well it scares me too.

Okay, so I'm warped beyond recognition, but I always was and the horses used to like that because they knew I didn't give a damn. That's the thing, that's the difference. Now I do care, because I've got to rope and ride with the best of them or else, what the hell will I do?

All I've ever wanted to do is ranch—ranch and get laid—but things sure do get deep around here with McKay feeling sorry for himself and Ted quietly going off his rocker, and Bobby fussing around like an old maid. Where the hell does that leave me? Maybe I ought to hire on elsewhere, but that's nothing new. Everyone keeps saying things have changed since the war, but hell, I think they're the same, except now all the dark corners show a little brighter. Bobby says McKay is like Prince Genji, whoever the hell that is—some romantic girl-chasing bastard from a thousand years ago. No telling what he calls me. We always did grate on each others' nerves. In fact I think I cause quite a bit of unhappiness around here. I go into town a lot. Now they're having regular dances again. So what if I limp, at least I've got two legs and something that hangs between them.

Today I got the colt in the round corral and stood in the middle leaning on my cane while he whirled around like something on the end of a rubber band. "Too much of this could make a man dizzy," I told him, trying to sound nonchalant. But I lied. I was madder than hell. Why didn't he just settle down? Then I thought I'd try something I'd seen Pinkey do—sit down in the middle of the corral and close my eyes like I was sleeping. Get real relaxed, then the colt would lose his fear. He trotted around, then finally I heard him stop. I peered through the slits of my eyes and saw him with his rump toward me, looking over his shoulder to see if I was cheating. And I was. He threw his head over the top rail, whinnied, then started trotting again.

I guess I lost my patience. I didn't have all day. Got up off my ass and kicked dirt at him. The colt jumped and tried to get away. "Jump again, damnit," I said, going toward him. You could scare a horse into standing still and that's what I was trying to do. As I got closer, he did stand, nervous and twitching, with his ears laid back listening to my footsteps. The muscle in his shoulder was shaking. When I got almost close enough to touch him, I watched to see if he would cock a back leg and fire at me. "Fire away. I'm used to it," I said. "I've been fired on by worse than you." But what good does bragging do with a horse? He dug in, spun, and ran spraying me with clods of dirt. I spit and wiped my face, thinking of the beach where I had been under fire, watching ammunition hit the sand, blasting it into the air, then when I was hit, it felt like sand had been driven all through me, my veins and bones, like human slurry, the stinging mixed up with the deep cold of pain.

The colt had been trotting but finally stopped. He was blowing pretty hard and sweat spread up his neck from his shoulder. "What in the hell buggered you, anyway?" It was an honest question. He laid his ears back in response. Was he laughing at me or was he just pissed? I leaned back on my cane because my leg hurt—there were snow clouds coming in—and breathed deeply. After, the horse sighed, then worked his mouth a little. He was relaxing. "That's good, Blue," I said. When I thought about it, I could feel how tense I'd been. "A horse knows even before you come out to catch him," Pinkey always said. But hell, you can't be perfect all the time, can you?

The thing is I'd had about enough. My little brother, Prince Charming McKay, gives me grief about my taste in women, about my pool game, about my roping, about, for god's sake, my morals, and Bobby is after me about getting married, and now this horse. What is it about me that he didn't like? From a horse it's different, it really gets to me because I thought we were pals, I thought all horses liked me.

Funny how something like this can get you down—a horse that won't be caught . . . Once I got close enough to touch his shoulder, but when I slid my hand up his neck holding the halter, rope, he pulled away. "You sonofabitch," I yelled as he flew by. The second time around I stuck my cane out, and he fired at me with a back leg, almost got me in the face. He jerked to a stop on his front feet, and I threw my cane, end over end. It hit him square on the hocks and broke in two. He lunged at the gate, breaking the top rail and the middle one. Then he jumped through and ran, across the irrigation ditch, out into the horse pasture. In the distance I could see McKay on a horse watching me. "Go screw yourself," I yelled to him, though he probably couldn't hear me. He rode away. Some present he'd given me. He must have trained this horse to run from me so everyone could laugh.

From my bedroom window the next morning I saw McKay run my colt back into the round corral and leave him there. "Shithead," I said, then slept some more. But what I saw when I went out there broke my heart: the colt's front legs were wirecut and swollen.

This time he stood. He worked his ears as I approached but didn't move a muscle. The game was over, but I had lost. I knelt, running my hand down one mangled leg. "Jesus, Blue, what the hell did you get so scared for?" But it was me who had been scared, not of the horse, but of my own incompetence, scared of this everlasting limp.

Went to the house for medicine and when I came back he had something in his mouth. I'll be goddamned if it wasn't a piece of my cane he was packing around like a puppy. When I went close to doctor his legs he touched his muzzle to my hand, and as I crouched down beside him, talking softly, he dropped the piece of cane on top of my bad knee as if to say, "That's what it's for, dummy, not for me."

After doctoring him for a month, I never did have trouble catching him again.

10

M c K A Y

THE DAY AFTER Pinkey's funeral I had the Rural Electric lineman come out to the ranch and hook us back up to electricity. I was tired of dim rooms and old-fashioned ways. That had to do with the war years and the strange happiness I felt, with the way having less turns into surfeit, and the crazy love was offered and taken without thought for the next day. Now I'm trying to get a new start with my brothers home and in the absence of Pinkey, Madeleine and Mariko, and I thought having things lit up a little brighter might be one way.

But this morning the lights went off. Bobby and I fiddled with the switch and the fuse but to no avail. We called the lineman and he came back out only to say nothing was wrong because when he flicked the switch, the lights came on. Later, Bobby heard a crash in the dining room: a window had blown open and all the bottles in the liquor cabinet had tipped sideways. This evening the lights went out again. Bobby, Champ, Ted, and I were eating when the room went dark. "The sonofabitch is haunted," Champ finally said, pushing his chair back from the table. I got up to look around but what was there to look for? Then I found that one of the fuses was dead, so I replaced it and we had lights again.

Just before I went to bed that night I had an idea. I went to the liquor cabinet, poured a shotglass of Cobb's Creek and set it out on the table because I had the distinct feeling that Pinkey was messing around. "How can you be so much trouble even when you're dead?" I asked aloud looking heavenward which was probably the wrong direction to look, and from that night on I always kept the whiskey glass filled.

That was the first night of the big storm, hard winds filled with snow. Forty inches fell in the first week followed by twenty more, followed by seven, then ten. Snow up to the window sills and drifts higher than my shoulder, smoothed and hardened so I could walk right over the tops of them. Had to doze out lanes for the cattle, lanes to water, lanes to the house and barn and corrals. Nights were hard. I felt cooped up, only these weren't necessarily the people I wanted to be cooped up with, not after what I'd had, not after Madeleine and Mariko. Sometimes I'd walk at night down long tunnels of snow, talk to the horses, or stand in the barn and look out over the white world below. "I almost had a child." That's what I found myself saying one night. What I meant, of course, was the child I had fathered with

Madeleine which she had lost while riding—years ago. I was sure it was a girl which pleased me because it meant I'd have two Madeleines in my life. At the same time, no day went by without thinking of Mariko.

How many years has my heart been split like this— split in two like a dowser's rod—hunting—bending down over hidden water? Mariko wrote from Paris. She sent photographs of her new paintings with a note attached—anything more would have been incriminating: She would have had to talk about feelings. This, from a woman who jumped out of a moving train and walked back ten miles to make love to me in an open field in view of the highway, our fingers smearing mud over each other so that after, we looked as if we had painted ourselves. And at parting—no words, no promises, no goodbyes, just those mud marks, those scars.

Now snow has covered all that. It's weight has suffocated even Pinkey's beyond-the-grave escapades. Ted is housebound, studying to go back to medical school, and Champ—the "human bomb"—as we like to call him because of his temper, has settled down to braiding rawhide reins like so much occupational therapy. But a step forward is a step forward. The day he broke his cane across his colt's hocks, sending him into the barbed wire, I felt the blow against my own legs as though he'd hit me. Five canes later—canes he broke over the backs of

127

chairs, over his own knee—his fury gradually subsided and now we work together feeding hay from a wagon pulled by a team with no more and no fewer resentments and quarrels than we had before the war.

Pleasure is never a constant thing. It surges through me as if my body were a hollow piece of straw. And so it was the few times Madeleine came to see me that winter. I couldn't help but notice she was more attractive than ever, her long copper braid intertwined with streaks of gray. I grabbed her, twirled her, went down on my knees, put my head against her and listened. Her stomach growled. "I'm hungry," she said laughing. "You always make me hungry."

I cooked for her. She watched me breaking eggs one-handed into a pan, cutting bread for toast, stoking the cookstove fire. Once her turquoise eyes filled with tears, then dried. "How's it going?" I asked. She twirled her wedding ring. She said everything bewildered her. "Maybe it would have been better if Henry had died. He's suffering so . . ."

When I touched her face she batted my hand away. "Stop trying to ruin my life," she snapped. We stood facing each other. "I'm not," I said. "I'm not trying anything." She spread her hands against my chest pushing, then pulling me toward her. "I'm not trying anything," I said again. I was in her arms and her head was against my chest. "Your heart beats irregularly," she said to me.

That was the last time I saw her until New Year's Eve when Bobby invited her and Henry for dinner. All morning he decorated the house with sprigs of pine and some white flowers he'd forced into bloom. Champ's girlfriend had already arrived and she lurked about the house when they weren't in the sack together. She didn't have much to say for herself and I was glad because I didn't feel like talking. Ted and Bobby cooked while Champ and I fed cows then we took our weekly baths.

When Madeleine and Henry came to the front door I couldn't help suppress a wild grin. I had a bottle of champagne and some glasses in my hand and I poured them a drink on the spot to keep the tossing and turning of jealousy and pleasure from showing. Henry and I embraced. He still looked thin. "But hell, I'm on the gain, two-point-four pounds a day just like a steer," he said, spilling his champagne onto my shoulder. Madeleine's hair was down and loose like water mixed with sun and I thought of Mariko's waist-length hair like black bamboo. In the kitchen Henry's hand shook as he raised his glass: "*Kampai*," he said. "Welcome home," Bobby chimed in and when I told him he looked "damned good," his mouth pulled to one side. "Like hell I do," he said, then we broke into laughter.

After dinner we all danced a little bit, taking turns with the two women, then grouping together, Ted, Champ, his girlfriend, Madeleine, Henry and me, and sometimes Bobby. Just before midnight we went outside to toast the New Year. I was already drunker than I wanted to be and once, when I closed my eyes, the ground moved backwards from under my feet and I stumbled head-on into a juniper tree. Then and there I relieved myself and when I turned back I saw Madeleine and Henry kissing—a prolonged, passionate kiss— and beyond, framed by the living room window, Champ and his girl danced by.

I sat in the jeep parked near the tree and turned on the engine and lights. They were aimed right at Henry's back and I could see Madeleine waving to me over his shoulder like a Hollywood star. I released the clutch. The jeep bumped toward them, then I slammed on the brakes because I thought I saw Pinkey coming toward me, but just then, Champ came to the door and yelled, "Happy New Year," and when I looked back I couldn't see Pinkey anymore.

I let the jeep go forward again. Once I heard Madeleine yelling at me, then Henry stepped in front of me with his hands out until the hood touched his fingers and bent them. He pulled back and ran behind the juniper with me on his tail. I could hear Champ laughing. Around and around we went. Hell, I never got close enough to run him down.

When I woke I was fully clothed on top of my bed. I

held my hand over my eyes. The light hurt. It seemed to me that most of my life I'd left a space in my bed for someone else—for Mariko, for Madeleine, for someone who might marry me— but it was unoccupied still. For a long time I lay there listening—Madeleine and Henry were gone, Champ and his girl were probably else-where. I collapsed my weight into the unused part of the bed. How cold it felt against my groin. Holding a hand over my eyes I imagined a body under me—Mariko's, Madeleine's— and beside us, a child.

11

THE BABY

SNUFF AND I had to give up the child. People had warned us and we ignored them. But a baby does not come into your life the way this one did—abandoned by the Wild-man in the front seat of a car in our parking lot—without someone eventually coming for her. It meant the end for Snuff and me, at least for awhile. Everything we had together evaporated the moment the baby was taken from my arms. Why he fled like that, I'm not sure. Maybe he thought I had failed or had brought us both bad luck, or maybe he didn't love me as much as he loved the child.

It happened the night a rock or a tree branch broke the bar's porthole window. Dark clouds blew in across the dance floor. I'd been up all night walking the baby because the storm had scared her. When I heard a knock on the front door, I thought it was wind. Who ever knocks on a bar door? Then I saw the sheriff. I told him to come in. He'd been here plenty of times, drunk as the rest of us when he wasn't on duty, but he gave me a funny look, a scared look and after, I saw why. I saw who was behind him: the baby's mother and her father, the banker.

I held the child hard to my chest. No one spoke. Then the banker said, "Tell her," to his daughter. I think her name is Dierdre, I'm not sure, it wasn't something I ever tried to remember.

She stared at the baby. Nothing registered in her eyes, nothing like maternal love, not even curiosity, though I saw the skin below her right eye twitch.

"You tell her," the man repeated.

Finally she spoke, "I want my baby back."

Outside I heard a car drone by. The wind had stopped. I wasn't sure where the floor was, the wind had been the floor, and now in silence, I sank down.

I heard the sheriff say something, his voice like a tin can, and my mind rose and divided, a plant unfurling out of the muck.

"What?" I asked.

"I said we don't want any trouble."

Another car went by, then I heard the wind gust.

"Trouble? This isn't about trouble." I didn't know what I meant, what I should say next. My voice cracked. "Where's Leni?" I asked. That was the Wildman's name.

"I don't know," the girl, said her voice flat.

"Does he know you are here?"

The girl's father interrupted, "That's none of your business."

"Hold on here," the sheriff said. "I have a paper that says you have to give the kid back to its rightful mother."

I took the paper from his hand, crumpled it, then dropped it on the floor. The girl quickly retrieved it, flattening it on her thigh as if she did not quite believe the words.

I felt the floor come under my feet again. "We could work out visits. I mean, come over any time and play with her. She would like that. She would like you, she's a happy baby." I pulled the blanket down so the girl could see the baby's face. Maybe that was a mistake because after, the girl slipped her hands under the child and said, "Give her to me," even though my arms were locked tight.

The sheriff pried my fingers apart. After that I don't remember anything. I had been robbed and there was nothing left.

*   *   *

A week has gone by. I don't know exactly when Snuff took off. He said he had to work some things out for himself, but I think he went to find the Wildman. I stayed in bed a lot with my clothes on. I remember one thing he said to me, "This is what happens to people like us. We don't belong and nothing belongs to us."

All I know is that I loved her. How could I explain to

135

a banker that a child could be raised in a bar with more family spirit, more straightforward love than I've seen in many nicer places. We'd come such a long way, Snuff and me, making a life together. Now this ache in my arms and breasts, now this bar which fills and empties with people like us, people who have their joys and sorrows and mostly sorrows.

When the regulars come in I let them mix their own drinks. I've retreated to a back room I cleared out with a view of the mountains. Willard comes home every afternoon after work. Someone drives him now—I don't know who. When he discovered the baby was gone he went beserk, tearing the bed apart, pulling clothes out of the closets, pushing chairs and tables over, then he dumped all her toys on the barroom floor and I had to bribe him with good things to eat to get him back into my room with me, away from people who could see our misery.

Sometime that week I called Esther, the Mormon woman who had lent us the crib and clothes. Out of ten children she had lost two of her own, so she knew something of what I was going through. She didn't say much, just folded the baby's things quietly and as she was leaving, took a firm grip on my arm and said, "You call if you need me. Day or night," and I told her I would though I couldn't imagine what I would ask of her. I had liked the way she called our foundling "an extra blessing"—

their term for children born out of wedlock or late in life, in the last years a woman is still able to have a baby but is probably through wanting one.

Snuff and I had tried to have a baby but nothing took, nothing happened, and we didn't attempt to find out why. Like he said, we'd always been drifters, each of us, and we'd made it our business to take in drifters and I guess it wasn't in our province to create something of our own.

Now the days and nights are an elastic that keeps stretching wider and emptier as if trying to make room for something bigger than me. During the windstorm a stray cat showed up. I took it as a sign and gave him milk but as soon as the wind died down, he vanished.

The day Willard was off from work we sat in the back room and looked at magazines. Their pictures made me feel I was still a part of the world, not just a figment of desolation's mirage. A light snow fell. Willard made "drinks" — three kinds of soda, a dash of beer and a cherry in each glass. He watched as I swallowed the concoction and threw his arms around me when I told him how good it was. He hung from my neck like a baby. Then we thumbed through back issues of *Look* and *Life* and read stories about MacArthur in Japan, about a beauty contest, and a movie star, and a car maker, a zoo, and pictures of the final destruction of France, England and Germany.

When he got bored Willard sat straight in a chair holding his willow branch like a staff. I don't know who he thought he was—maybe someone from one of the magazines—but I told him he looked like a king. We squandered days and nights like this. He stopped going to work and I stopped going out into the bar. I didn't care who drank what or about money, but they paid anyway. I dragged blankets, quilts, sheets, and pillows into the little room and we ate what meals we had in there and slept on the floor. Sometimes I'd wake up with my head lying on an open page of *Life*, the lamps on, morning light coming through the window. One of those mornings my sister called. I told her the baby was gone, that there was no floor under my feet, that a boulder with sharp edges at the bottom of a hole where the baby had been dropped had lodged in my dreams, and she said I should talk to someone, that no one could go through a loss like this without help.

I shrieked with laughter. Talk to who? The priest, the postmaster, the sheriff? "If you mean some head-shrinker, we haven't got any of them here."

I never have asked for help. Goodness, what a thought. I mean straight out waltzed in and asked for it. I came to this bar, alright, but I never asked for anything. It was all Snuff's idea, me staying here and everything that came after, and now it's gone and there's nothing left to ask for. Anyway, I've got Willard.

"Are you listening? Willard, I'm talking." What's there to say? I've been around a little bit, I've been through some hard times I guess. "Willard?"

Why does my body feel like glass again, something that's to be broken open?

Willard smiles. I dive into the magazines again. More days go by. Sometimes little noises come up into his throat, a creaking hum as if he were trying to sing or speak. I put my ear to his throat. My hair tickles him. I've become so unkempt, my hair hanging in straight strings. Listen, Willard, you have to help me, you have to tell me what to do now, how to make the ache stop, you have to teach me to sleep without listening for the baby's cries, how to see whatever comes next in a life if there is anything.

The magazine falls open to a picture of an old man wearing glasses, listening to a woman opposite, lying on a couch. It is a "Dr. Jung," except he doesn't live any place close to this bend in the highway that comes from nowhere and leads to nothing. He couldn't hear me even if he wanted to.

Willard thumps his stick. If he is the king, then I am his servant I wait on him. More Coke, more jerky, a fried egg sandwich, no two. When I come back I have an idea. Willard eats while I push chairs together, four of them with a hard pillow at one end for my head and he sits opposite, listening. I lie down. Willard stares at me

139

from under heavy-lidded eyes and I try to begin. But something's missing: Willard needs glasses. Out in the bar I find some dark glasses with one lens cracked. "Here, wear these. Oh my god, you look like a blind man." Willard smiles. I lie down again. Like those glasses my life seems dark and cracked. I lie still, then hear myself yelling: "I want to get out of here, I want to drive, I want to go somewhere, I don't want to be me."

Willard's head falls forward in sleep. Didn't he hear me? I sob endlessly.

* * *

A scuffling sound woke me and the presence of someone near. When I opened my eyes I saw Snuff standing over me holding a baby fawn, so young even at this time of year, it still had spots on its flank.

"He's hungry," Snuff said. "I found him by the road."

Tears big as boulders rolled from his eyes.

12

VELMA VERMEER

THIS MORNING I put on the dress I was married in, a long chemise with slits on the sides made of stiff silk trimmed in silver sequins. It hangs on me now because I'm so thin. Isn't it usually the other way around: the petite bride growing into a fleshy monster? Slipped the dress right over my head and felt it race over my bones. Too much is revealed by the neckline. The cords of my neck protrude like long pull ropes on church bells. It's true that Harry and I loved to sing — anything from hymns to duets from Rigoletto, but now, of course, I sing alone. It's been six years since Harry took his life in the town's only movie theatre. Now I wonder, what's the use of having a voice . . . but what am I saying? That's how I make my living these days, as the telephone operator.

I hold my hand to the front of my throat. The songs I sing now are silent as if the years had rubbed the notes away. How awkward I look in this dress. Maybe I did then too. The switchboard buzzes; I put on my earphones. "Hello, this is Velma, can I help you?" I said,

141

though truly, I wasn't much in the mood to help anyone at all.

We were married at sea, Harry and I, as unlikely as that sounds now. Heavens, I haven't even seen an ocean for forty years. It was a spur of the moment thing since Harry and I had just met, fellow insomniacs, pacing the decks all night, circling round and round, passing each other until finally he took my arm at the elbow and we promenaded together from stern to bow.

Harry was on the short side, redheaded and rotund, and wore a necktie. At the end of that first night he didn't hold me or kiss me but ran his hands down the sides of my body and said, "God, you have a waist, a beautiful waist," and called me his "mermaid," then asked if I would go to the opera with him in Vienna.

Maybe it doesn't sound like much of a start but it was enough for me. Not the part about Vienna, but the way he naturally assumed I would be interested in such things and asked if he could undo three buttons on my cardigan and kiss my throat which, embarrassed, I let him do. That was a Monday and on Thursday at six o'clock sharp during the cocktail hour on the poop deck, we were married. The captain had announced it at breakfast, wiping toast crumbs from his lips with a linen napkin: "Everyone is invited," he said laconically, and some few did come.

Word went around among the women passengers that I needed something appropriate to wear and by noon on Tuesday the steward slipped a note under my door: "Come to Cabin 11B after luncheon. I might have something for you. Natalie Whitfield." I went at the appointed hour. My goodness, standing in the middle of her stateroom was a trunk packed with evening clothes.

"Come in my dear," she said in a whiskey voice, putting a cigarette to her lips. The diamond at her neck glittered. "Please help yourself." She could see I was too embarrassed to rifle through her belongings. Finally I held a dress up. "You must try it on," she ordered. "No way to know until you see for yourself, but I think you'll like this one," she said, pulling a silk chemise from the back of the trunk. I undressed in her bedroom as she fixed herself a drink. "A scotch?" she called out, but I said no. The dress fit perfectly. She zipped up the back and made me turn slowly. "Marvellous. Looks like it was made for you." She looked at my hair. "Don't you think it would be nice to pull it back like this and tie it with a bow?" she said, showing me. "And then you'll need something for around your neck." She laid out a satin jewelry case on her bed: pearls, diamonds, an emerald bracelet, rings and earrings. I had never seen such things. "The pearls and those earrings . . ." she said. "Do try them on . . . it would please me." There was a knock at the door. It was Harry. Gracious but

143

stern, Mrs. Whitfield said, "Don't be silly. You're not allowed to see the bride," and, winking at me, sent him away.

A bride. I had never thought of myself that way. Had no intention of marrying. I had a good job as secretary to a district court judge. What little I knew about life, I suppose I learned there, both the good and the bad, but mostly bad. My goodness, the things people do to one another . . . Well, reading through those cases was enough excitement for me. But Harry was in show business. That's what I learned about him in the intervening days until our wedding. Said he'd hung around backstage doors until they finally gave him a job, and worked himself up to the position of stage manager. Said he'd had an unhappy childhood in a small Wyoming town—mostly miners, including his father—a town where the Chinese had been massacred, a town where his interests had been neither understood nor tolerated. "If they didn't like the Chinese, why would they like me?" he said.

Thursday afternoon Mrs. Whitfield helped me dress. I was all thumbs and she insisted that everything be just right, as if I were her daughter. "I didn't have a daughter," she said. "Just one son and he isn't worth a damn." She made me wear the diamond earrings and pearl choker. Just before it was time to go up on deck she stepped back from me and said: "You look lovely. My husband and I eloped too. Best thing to do. To hell with these mob-scene society weddings . . ." though to be truthful, I wouldn't have minded one of those either. There was a knock at the door. "Harry?" I asked, but it was the captain. Before she opened the door she put her fingers to my neck. "You keep these. My wedding present to you, please." How could I say anything at a time like that? Speechless, I let the captain escort me up the stairs. I would return everything the next day. When Harry saw me his face went crimson. He looked round and jolly in his tuxedo. I noticed the sleeves were frayed. After that moment, I remember nothing of the ceremony except the captain slurred the words he read out of a tiny, battered prayerbook I suspected wasn't his.

After the wedding, Harry, Mrs. Whitfield and I sat at the Captain's table. Champagne, caviar, the works. Very festive. Later, there was a dance. We put flowers behind our ears and when the passengers cleared the floor for us, Harry and I waltzed clumsily and I heard a woman say, "Look she's taller than he is," which I was with high heels on.

"You look like a silver bell," Harry said to me. "Like a thousand full moons." Such words! What could I possibly say in response? Later, I remember him taking the dress from me—raising it over my head then running his hands down my ribs and waist and hips saying those words again: "My mermaid."

145

"If you can have just this one time of great happiness in your life." I remember Mrs. Whitfield saying sometime during the evening, "Then whatever happens doesn't matter." I told that to Harry as we lay together in the moonlight. I knew I was rather homely and provincial, so it pleased me when he said yes and that I was beautiful and smiled.

Near dawn the ship's siren sounded. We dressed hurriedly and went on deck. "MAN OVERBOARD! MAN OVERBOARD!" the loudspeaker blared. We ran from one side of the ship to the other, searching the wrinkled sea. Floodlights poured over black water. Nothing. Lifeboats were readied. Harry kissed me, then let himself be lowered. How I hated to see him vanish down the side of the ship like that, but the steward came rushing by and told me who was missing: it was Mrs. Whitfield.

I couldn't believe it was she. My friend. When Harry returned, what seemed like hours later, his face was ashen. "She's gone," he said, and I could see the black swells that had lifted him back to me had already stained our lives.

13

BOBBY'S CABIN

THE FIRST NIGHT I found Ted unconscious behind my cabin I thought he was asleep. My lantern threw its boxed light across his legs. Couldn't rouse him. Clothes — wet all through and with the wind putting cold air into the hot sky, had to get him inside. Put something under his nose to wake him up, then pulled him onto my bed and covered him with a blanket. Made him drink some tea, and he slept.

Guess that's what the noises I'd heard were. Thought it was a deer or a skunk. Had he been trying to get to my cabin? Had he been coming to see me? All I know is this: the day he came home from the war I could see his spirit was thin, thin as a wafer and I didn't know if it would hold. What medicine do I give for the spirit? I wondered. When he came to, he said he felt as if his feet never touched the ground, they hung between his hips and the planet, swinging. The doctors said his inner ear had been punctured. Maybe so. Maybe that's where his spirit is draining from. It came oozing out from somewhere like sap and no one could see it but me. In the morning he didn't say a word, just got up and ran home.

The first thing I did this year when spring came, the spring after the end of the war, was to take down the barbed wire handrail on the little bridge between my cabin and the ranch house, and make a new one of pine poles which I peeled and planed smooth. In the mornings on the way to make breakfast for the boys, I like to stand on the bridge and listen to the water. It reminds me of the slender red bridge in my home village, what my mother referred to as *yume no ukihashi* – the floating bridge of dreams that could take us from this life to another. I used to laugh at that. "But mother, look, I've walked across, does that mean I'm in heaven?" She made a hissing sound, but now that I am near my own end, I don't laugh about it anymore.

How many times I've stood on this bridge. The barbed wire was one of Pinkey's jokes, but it was bad, nothing to put your hands on. Now the smooth wood arches under my palms like a bow flexing, the whole of my life flying like a fortune out of the palm of my hand. The bridge separates my world from the world of the boys, my traditions from theirs. Now one of them, Ted crosses over at night and comes to me.

When Ted came next I wasn't surprised. *Ofuro* all ready, made him get in; above, the full moon with the side chopped off and the face that looked down on us pitilessly. He said nothing, just did what I said. I watched him from inside the cabin. Sometimes I wasn't sure if he would survive, I could see the wafer of his spirit was like the moon behind shadow—there and not there.

In my village we used to take our bathtubs down to the river and fill them right there, then build a fire with driftwood. All along the river you could see neighbors bathing this way in the evenings. We didn't have plumbing or bathrooms and in good weather, this was easier than carrying water to the house and heating it there.

After his bath, Ted wrapped himself in a big towel and came inside. Made him sit on the bed and smell the flowers. I believe we sometimes overlook simple remedies. Flowers are good for the spirit. In our village, the smell of orange blossoms went everywhere. He didn't say much. Outside, wild stars all matted together, the whole sky white. Then he said, "Please tell me a story." I suppose that's what he used to ask of his parents when he was a boy and they were around, but they are gone, only me left of the old ones.

It's funny, he didn't really know anything about my life and I knew everything about his. But now his feet have been on my soil, on Japanese ground, and I suppose that's why he wanted to know. A breeze blew through the south window. *Kamisama* coming to help me. "That wind comes from Japan," I told him, "the same wind that blew my ship here from Osaka to San Francisco."

"Ship was bad. Lied about my age to get on. Was I fourteen, fifteen, sixteen? Somewhere in there. Slept on deck. Bad smell below. Mostly men coming from Hiroshima-ken, poor farmers like my family, coming to America to make money to send home. Now every one knows Hiroshima, but not in those days. My village is north of there and back in the mountains where it is beautiful. But we had to sell our rice to buy other things we needed. Ate rice mixed with barley, rice with pickles, and sometimes tiny trout I caught with my hands in the stream. And the neighbors let me take the fruit that had fallen to the ground—*mikan* and persimmons—but that's all.

"Our village was six hundred years old. In old days, it was a way station for samuri who had to go to the capital, and they stayed in the bigger houses in the village, not ours. I took care of their horses. But we were so poor I heard my mother crying at night under the covers, so another boy and I went away, went north to an uncle's pickle factory, but it was very bad there, so I came here.

"It was a long trip for boys who didn't know where they were going or what they would do when they got here. Many days, maybe a month went by, then one day I smelled land, saw seagulls and diving ducks, cormorants, and smelled guano, trees and grass. Next

150

morning, woke up suddenly because didn't feel the wind. Looked around. We were in the Bay. Heard fog horns. What funny music they have here, I thought. Then on the docks saw people who looked like dogs, with funny eyes and all colors of hair.

"They took us in at Angel Island, all mixed in with the Chinese. Some of them had been there for a month, but I was Japanese, I was healthy and learned English on the ship from sailor who learned it in India. So I said those words I learned to the officers. Maybe not always the right ones, but they let me through.

"Made my way to Chinatown where Japanese lived too. Oh my, the things I saw, not like anything at home . . . Bad place. Narrow alleys with women living in them, not geisha, but women who went with men for money, and these were Japanese women too. There were three kind: Women who went with Japanese men only, women who went with Chinese, women who went with Americans. Do you know why? Because Japanese man would not sleep with woman who had been with Chinese man, and so on . . . it was to keep the races straight. So that's why when I saw those signs around here that said, NO JAPS, I wasn't surprised. All this hatred is everywhere.

"I slept in Chinatown hotel for Japanese only. Washed dishes to pay rent. Oh, that food smelled so good, like I had never left home. Next morning went to place

151

where I could apply for job. Up on big blackboard were things we could do: houseboy, farm hand, miner, railroad crew. I was small and not very strong-looking so man asked if I could cook. I lied and said yes. He sent me off to Union Pacific office and next day went out with all Chinese crew. Chinese thought that was funny, because man didn't know the difference between one nationality and the other. But I didn't care. Only thing was, I didn't know how to cook for Chinese. Old man helped me. Americans had dining car. We didn't. We cooked food on the side of the tracks, fried up all these things in big woks, very greasy, but tasted good. We worked through the mountains, across the desert where it was so hot—couldn't eat during the day, had dinner at midnight. Worked across Utah, saw where the Mormons had come to live, then into Wyoming, and that's how I came to be here."

When I finished my story, Ted lay back with his hands behind his head. His hospital ship had been hit by a torpedo and he got shrapnel in his head. The bandages had only recently been removed and for a long time I studied the dent in his skull where hair was just beginning to grow. He said the inside of his head still felt like a broken egg, but he let me touch the wound.

Then we went outside and sat on the little bridge with our feet hanging over rushing water and looked at the stars. The village where I was from was called "Beautiful

Stars." There were so many of them we could not pick out the constellations. It was like the stories, he said, there were so many of them to tell.

I could see he was quiet inside. Maybe his spirit had begun to heal. Stories do that to people, they make us forget ourselves. That night I felt a little lost. I had not thought of these things for a long time, these tales, all bound up—a closed book—until Ted started coming to my cabin, and now, night after night, page after page, they fly from me.

14

TED'S NIGHT

SOMETIME . . . WAS IT this morning? . . . I unwound the last bandage from my head. There's a dent above my eye that goes back into the hairline where they had to go in and dig out shrapnel. Now I'm lying naked on Bobby's bed. He found me wandering. Got wet in the rain. Funny, I haven't been in here since I was a little boy. I think it's night now, but I don't know which night, and it doesn't matter. How did he know I was out there? No dogs barked. He grabbed my shirt collar like he used to do when I was a kid and spun me around, then led me inside and made me drink something awful, some healing potion because he says my spirit is dead.

When I was lying wounded on that ship in the Pacific someone had to hold me down. Think it was the dentist . . . like he was going to drill my teeth or something. Straddled my legs and pinned my shoulders to the deck, then he put his hand into the hole in my head—maybe he was trying to read my mind—and I saw the blood. Doctors aren't supposed to get hurt, that's all I could think.

Earlier we had passed a ship that had been torpedoed and there were men in the water, calling for help. I stood on deck waiting to feel the engine vibrations die down and the slow sliding stop of the ship so we could lower life rafts and pick the men out of the drink, but we kept going right past them. I ran to the bridge.

"Can't stop," the first mate said, grabbing my arm. "We're not a hospital ship."

"I don't care what the hell we are . . ."

That first mate and I struggled, but I knew it was useless. Back down on deck I watched our wake slosh over those men. The water was red where they were floating. I vomited.

Next thing I knew I was laid out flat on the deck in a pool of my own blood. That's why we hadn't stopped, I guess. We were dodging torpedoes. My head didn't hurt. I felt like a bird that had flown into a window—stunned. I tried to get up. I remember the time on Dad's ranch in Mexico when a mean bull got loose and knocked a bunch of the hired men down. They were lying all over the field. One was gored and bleeding. I was just a kid and the sight made me laugh—not because I was more callow than the next kid, but because it looked so odd. And that rank old bull kept trotting around the pasture looking for someone else to knock down.

155

God, Bobby, my head . . . it's not like a stabbing pain but a dull planetary roar, then sloshing as if ocean water had been poured into both ears.

There, that's good. What is it? Something smells good. Flowers? They make the sloshing stop. The fragrance rises above the ache. So much pressure in there still, but there's space at the top for perfume.

* * *

I'm still naked. I can feel that. It's warm in the room and Bobby has a fire going in the woodstove. He comes over and touches the dent in my skull. Rubs some kind of ointment there. My hair is beginning to grow back. I'm supposed to return to med school in three weeks to begin my residency. But not yet. I can't. I've got to sleep. Can't look into those mansions of suffering, those bodies . . . I've got to sleep.

When Bobby lays a blanket over me, I feel the wool against my skin and remember thinking on the ship that I might not have any skin, that it had exploded and peeled away with the noise of the blast. Now I don't have skin but scar tissue.

Scars are like eyes that register nothing. Something may have happened but nothing is revealed. It is a place on the body where history has been erased, but someone bungled the job. The marks of passage are still there—smooth and numb, numb and itching, aching . . .

Like ice. Yes. There. Touch it again. No, don't.

Peter's dead, did I tell you that, Bobby? Not in action but before we shipped out. Got a letter from his girlfriend—you know what I mean—I mean she was screwing his best friend. He would have been a good doctor. He had a big heart, maybe too big. We were in Italy. He read this letter, then jumped down the stairwell.

Bobby, can I go now? I don't want to talk. Come here. Sit down and tell me a story.

* * *

I think I slept. Bobby is curled up on the floor in front of the fire. I dreamed my head bandage was being taken off—two doctors unwinding and unwinding. Blood all over the place. They were talking about a patient. Why they did one procedure and not the other, why they lost him. My bandage kept unrolling. When they came to the end of it, I realized it was my skin and I was dead.

Bobby, am I running? There's a soft rain, a female rain. I'm running into its face, through its body. Can't someone hold me?

I see Bobby's face come close to mine. What is he looking at? Something way back behind my eyes. He smooths my bedcovers. On the ship, after I knew I still had skin, I wasn't sure if there was a body left, anything below the neck.

My skin is unwinding. I think of Gloria, who was my girl. These blanket are so smooth. I look down and see the outlines: chest, stomach, cock, knees, toes. In a dream, someone had drawn an outline of me on a wall. A sculptor handing up palms full of flesh, pressing them between the lines. Is that how a body is made? My cock stirs a little, answering, yes.

Bobby brings another drink. This one is gooseberry juice, mint and burdock root. It tastes sweet and of the earth at the same time. Why does he bother with me? He pulls up a three-legged stool and sits, bent over. The fire throws his shadow up, and the log wall makes it ripple. "You look like a glass of water, Bobby."

Give me a drink, please. Not that shit, something strong and real. Strong and real because my body is going even though Bobby says my spirit is sick, that's all I have left. The spirit viscous but transparent.

This blanket is the only thing holding me in. It's not that I'm made of water, but . . . look, I can remember blood spilling across the gray deck like lava. The deck fire made my skin burst. I remember swimming inside a volcano, in the arms of a caldera where the lava was blue.

* * *

Bobby, something in my neck is burning. Now the lights in the room are out. On ship, that's when I could always sleep, when the shorelights had receded and I was tossed by rough seas into oblivion.

Gloria, where are you? Aren't we already married with kids on the way? Can't you put a hand here to stave off this leaking body of mine, stop the skin from slipping away?

* * *

Raining still . . . Drumming the tin roof like someone playing with bones above my head. Do I have clothes on? Legs? I'm afraid to reach my hand down . . . if it comes back with blood . . .

Bobby, did I tell you I was the only one to know what the word *kamikaze* meant?. Our ship wasn't torpedoed. A plane flew into the foredeck. They said the Shinto priests who gave the *kamikaze* pilots their farewell blessing wore robes of diaphanous white as if the young men had already died and were in heaven.

Now I know what it's like to be dead. There's a great humming and the deck of the ship is like ice and something warm trickles from both ears and the body is made of balsa wood . . .

Bobby tells me a story about a love-suicide where two lovers made a pact and died together in crashing waves. "That way, you are not lonely when you die," he says. But how could anyone go through with it if your eyes were locked on your lover's because that's what life is about—locking eyes with the world.

"Too romantic," I say.

When Bobby doesn't agree, he tips his head to one side and sucks in breath. "Ohhhh . . ." he growls, which means he's not so sure.

But even surety, like the body, is illusion.

* * *

Bobby rips the blanket off. I'm wet from sweating. Didn't I hear someone scream? He takes a damp towel and wipes me off. I turn on my stomach. He brings the towel down my back, over my buttocks, down my legs, touching the bottoms of my feet.

Out the window I see the sun rise.